MAY   2016   TEEN

D0428637

CONCENTR8

Day One

For Darren, wherever you are

Also by William Sutcliffe

The Wall

CONCENTR8

CONCENTR8

WILLIAM SUTCLIFFE

BLOOMSBURY
NEW YORK LONDON OXFORD NEW DELHI SYDNEY

First published in Great Britain in August 2015 by Bloomsbury Publishing Plc
Published in the United States of America in January 2016
by Bloomsbury Children's Books
www.bloomsbury.com

Bloomsbury is a registered trademark of Bloomsbury Publishing Plc

For information about permission to reproduce selections from this book, write to
Permissions, Bloomsbury Children's Books, 1385 Broadway, New York, New York 10018
Bloomsbury books may be purchased for business or promotional use.
For information on bulk purchases please contact Macmillan Corporate and
Premium Sales Department at specialmarkets@macmillan.com

Library of Congress Cataloging-in-Publication Data
Names: Sutcliffe, William.
Title: Concentr8 / by William Sutcliffe.
Other titles: Concentrate
Description: New York : Bloomsbury Children's Books, 2016.
Summary: Through multiple perspectives, tells of London in the near
future where, when the government stops distributing a behavioral modification
drug, Concentr8, chaos erupts and five teens take a man hostage, seemingly
at random, changing all of their lives forever.
Identifiers: LCCN 2015022807
ISBN 978-1-61963-919-5 (hardcover) • ISBN 978-1-61963-920-1 (e-book)
Subjects: | CYAC: Hostages—Fiction. | Kidnapping—Fiction. | Conduct of life—
Fiction. | Gangs—Fiction. | London (England)—Fiction. | England—Fiction. | BISAC:
JUVENILE FICTION/Action & Adventure/General. | JUVENILE FICTION/Law &
Crime. | JUVENILE FICTION/Social Issues/General (see also headings under Family).
Classification: LCC PZ7.S9666 Co 2016 | DDC [Fic]—dc23
LC record available at http://lccn.loc.gov/2015022807

Typeset by Integra Software Services Pvt. Ltd.
Printed and bound in USA by Berryville Graphics Inc., Berryville, Virginia
2 4 6 8 10 9 7 5 3 1

All papers used by Bloomsbury Publishing, Inc., are natural, recyclable products made
from wood grown in well-managed forests. The manufacturing processes conform to the
environmental regulations of the country of origin.

Attention Deficit Hyperactivity Disorder is supposed to affect up to 10 per cent of young children (mainly boys). The 'disorder' is characterised by poor school performance and an inability to concentrate in class or to be controlled by parents, and is supposed to be a consequence of disorderly brain function...The prescribed treatment is an amphetamine-like drug called Ritalin. There is an increasing world-wide epidemic of Ritalin use. Untreated children are said to be likely to be more at risk of becoming criminals.

Steven Rose, *The 21st Century Brain*

TROY

You want to know how I got famous? This is how.

I wasn't proper famous. Didn't last more than a few days. I wasn't popular famous neither. I mean, most famous is we-love-you famous or you-done-something-good famous—this was the opposite. For a few days me and Blaze and the others were the official scumbags of the universe. But what I'm saying is—we ain't. We ain't and we weren't.

Taking a guy off the street, tying him to a radiator, and keeping him sounds psycho, but if you knew me—if you knew my whole life and what happened up to that day—you'd get it. I mean, you probably still wouldn't like me—so what, that don't mean nothing anyway—but you'd know I ain't crazy or evil or any of that other stuff they said about me.

Don't nobody want to see it that way, though. Not now. Listen, it started when London was totally flipped—I mean, the whole city had just gone mental—lost it—and I'm not saying I knew what was going to happen, but when things did kick off I wasn't surprised. It was the way the madness got so big so fast—the way everyone took it up—the way the police seemed to give in and leave us to it, that's what was so wild. It's like suddenly anything was allowed, literally anything—stuff you can't even imagine till it's right there in front of you. Stealing, burning, smashing places up; and that's just the start—'cause when you actually see looting with your own eyes it's hard to believe—it's insane. Sort of like all the shops are open and everything's free and people are just losing their minds—running in, taking whatever they can carry, and running out again with a look on their face that says *This can't be happening but it is!*

When they took away Concentr8 they must have known it was like shaking up a Coke can and flipping the ring tab—they knew it but they didn't care, and blaming us for what we did is like blaming the Coke for squirting you in the face. They made it happen, so there ain't no excuse for them acting all surprised.

In those last few normal days we all knew something was different, like when the air goes thick before a storm. You could feel it everywhere. In the projects—in the streets—just looking in the eyes of other kids there was a crackle like everyone knew all it would take was one spark to set the whole place on fire.

I missed the beginning, but people are saying now it's the kids who started it—going mad for Concentr8—but then on the second night all them other people angry about all them other things joined in and it just rolled on—got bigger and bigger till it felt like it was everyone out there on the streets howling it out like wild dogs—letting rip—everything bursting out, just a river of anger flooding from everywhere so nothing could stop it. Funny thing is, when anger comes out—when it's been boxed up and boxed up then it explodes—it feels like a happy thing, like a celebration, like a party—don't know why, it just does. It's like anger and the opposite of anger mixed together out there on the streets tearing it up—half party, half war.

If you opened all the doors on all the cages at London Zoo you'd get the exact same thing—playtime for the animals, and everyone else shitting bricks. It'd be the zookeepers that'd get eaten first—ain't that the truth.

There was one moment—and this was later, after what I'm trying to tell you about—one moment when me and Blaze were walking along and it was early evening. Things were just getting going and we had our bandanas around our necks— not up yet, but ready for when things started—and there was this guy sitting in a restaurant eating a meal. He saw us walking past and he looked at us the way people like that always do—with a sneering kind of disgust on his face like just our clothes and the way we walk make us scum. I don't go out of my yard much—ain't safe—but if we do, we get that look all the time and we're used to it, so I didn't even notice anything unusual. Blaze is different, though. He saw that look just like I did—but he knew the feds were busy—knew everything was going crazy and there was no rules no more—all that shit was on pause—and he lifted a foot and kicked the window in. Just like that. Karate style with his heel. The glass shattered and fell everywhere on the floor onto the guy's table, onto his plate and over his lap, and you should have seen the look on his face. Like he couldn't believe what just happened—like he thought he was about to die—like one minute he's watching a war movie on TV, then suddenly the TV explodes and guys burst out firing real guns at him.

It was beautiful. He felt so safe behind that glass, then suddenly, quick as it takes to flick off a light, he realized that anything could happen to him—that he wasn't in a different world looking down on us from miles up—we were right there in front of him in the same place and if we wanted to, we could jump through the broken window and do anything. I swear, one minute he's the big man in a suit eating his fancy meal, then the next second he's like a naked baby quivering, totally helpless, not a clue in his head what's going to happen to him—more scared than you ever seen anyone.

For a second we looked at each other through the jaggedy hole—all three stuck in position by the madness of what just happened. I stood there feeling the buzz—a waft of chilled restaurant air brushing my hot cheeks—then we just laughed and walked off, leaving that guy in front of his glass-covered meal probably sitting in a puddle of his own piss. The look on his face—funniest thing I ever seen.

It was Blaze who told me it was starting—Blaze who messaged me to get off my ass and come taste the magic. I go around his place and I thought he'd be pumped like me, but he's calm—chilling in his room. It's even hotter in there than outside—the air sweet and thick with smoke and heavy like every mouthful has been breathed over and over. He fills me in—tells me he was out the night before when things flipped and how gangs of kids squared off to the feds chucking stuff, on and on half the night and how he thought that was it—but now it's all going off again but bigger, much bigger, and I got to see it. It's wild and beautiful, he says. Those are the words he uses. Wild and beautiful.

He reminds me to be careful, to keep my bandana up, to stay away from cameras, to avoid anywhere I might be cornered. No dead-end streets, no shops without a back door. He asks me what I want. Sneakers? Phones? He says it with a smirk like he's messing with me and I feel like any answer will sound stupid, so I just bounce the question back at him. That's when he tells me he's got a plan—says he's going to do something big and asks me if I want to join him.

When Blaze asks you a question like that, it ain't really a question. You can't say no—nobody says no to Blaze. Not 'cause we're scared of him—at least I ain't—but because you just want to go where he goes and do what he does. The alternative is to be in the wrong place away from the action. Ain't no option but to go along for the ride. I don't even say nothing, but he knows I'm in.

When we set off from Blaze's apartment it ain't even dark yet, but there's already people streaming back into the projects carrying armfuls of stuff. There's one guy with a stack of Foot Locker shoeboxes up to his chin and he's trying to run but he can't. He drops one but doesn't even stop for it. We call after him but he just says we can have them.

We have a look, but they're the wrong size and a shit brand, so we head on. There's people with heaps of clothes still on hangers. There's a lady with three huge boxes of detergent. There's others hauling wheelie bins filled with god knows what but so heavy it takes two to pull—all surging in on a hot wind funneling through the towers almost like off a hand dryer. A bloke goes past with three plastic bags in each hand stuffed with cigarettes—all wild eyes and a massive grin like he can't believe his luck.

I want to run before everything goes. I can't believe we're only a bit late and already it feels like all the good stuff might have gone—but Blaze doesn't even quicken his step, so I stay with him 'cause it's Blaze—and fact is, me and him are always side by side. Now more than any other day I don't want to lose him. Ain't saying I need him—just saying we're a team, stronger together 'cause some places, whoever you are, you ain't safe on your own.

Blaze must have been messaging the others, 'cause there's six of us altogether by the time we walk out into the unbelievable mayhem on the high street—into the drifting smoke—into the nonstop wail of more sirens than you can count—alarms ringing everywhere—breaking glass— surges of shouting and cheering as something catches fire or smashes or as a new shutter gets lifted. Just the minute you smell it and hear it, you know you ain't never felt proper chaos till now. Gives you a tingle as you walk into it—like some incredible movie coming alive all around you in 3D and you're actually in it—able to pick stuff up and touch and throw and run. It's like all your life you know what's fantasy and what's solid, then suddenly you find yourself in a place where the two are mashed up together and you don't know what's what—'cause however much you stare and blink, this kind of shit just don't seem real.

I seen end-of-the-world stuff on DVD hundreds of times. Every other movie you see ends with something like this. But now I know they got it wrong every single time, 'cause I ain't never heard no sound like this—ain't never heard nothing so wild that kicks you in the stomach with some weird kind of terror that you got to run toward, not away from. It's huge, it swallows you up, this sound of every single person out on the street knowing there ain't no police, no fear, no consequences, and you can do anything.

Never even realized half the things you ain't allowed to do till I saw what it looks like when suddenly everyone can do whatever they want. It's something you got to see to believe and I swear if you die without ever living it, that's almost as bad as dying a virgin.

So the six of us walk along—feeling it, swimming in it, with our eyes bulging out at the craziness everywhere. No cars, just people on the streets with bandanas up, covering their faces and even though it's insane, everyone seems to know where they're going. People are running. People are carrying piles of stuff from the shops—pushing whole TVs around in supermarket carts—just staggering with bags and bags of shit from everywhere with spaced-out drugged-up eyes as if looting is the biggest high they ever had.

It looks like Foot Locker's the first place everyone's gone for. The shutter's twisted up, bent to one side, and inside it's been picked bare—you can see the last people coming out all disappointed 'cause there ain't nothing left.

Next door five blokes are trying to take out a cash machine. A few doors down from that there's a swarm of people heaving at a metal grille over the door of Currys. They're going at it with crowbars and hammers and bricks and even a plank of wood. One guy's shouting at everyone, trying to get them organized to work together, but half the people are ignoring him and just trying to batter it in. Three guys together are dropping a paving stone again and again onto the padlock. There's a cheer as it snaps. The shutter goes up and the doors give way a few seconds later. Like water down the drain, people flood in, pushing against each other— elbows and fists everywhere. It gets a bit nasty when people start running out with boxes of TVs and laptops and printers while more people are trying to fight their way in. A woman gets knocked over and a few people coming out just tread on her—maybe 'cause they can't see over what they're carrying or maybe because they don't give a shit. Someone pulls the woman off the ground and punches a guy who trod on her and a fight starts, but most people just ignore the fight and go around it—in and out of the shop.

Blaze ain't moved. He stares just calm like normal—no excitement, no panic, nothing—cold hard eyes watching everything, but his whole body totally still—not even a flicker—and 'cause he ain't going in, none of us do it either.

Eventually Karen says, *What are we waiting for?*

So quiet you can hardly even hear it over all the noise Blaze just says, *Go if you want.*

Nobody moves.

Look at this shit, says Femi. *There's everything!*

Go ahead, says Blaze.

Femi looks at Karen and she looks back at him, but they don't leave.

If we just stay everything'll be gone. Are we going to just watch everyone else get it all? says Jay.

I ain't a thief, says Blaze. I don't know why he says that, 'cause he is—I mean, not often, but we all done it sometimes. Ain't easy to contradict Blaze, though, so I know nobody's going to say, *Yes you is.*

They steal from us! says Jay.

Who does?

It's a weird conversation because we're all standing in a line not looking at one another, just staring straight ahead, watching a huge shop being emptied out by swarms of people. The look of disbelief on their faces as they come out carrying armfuls of stuff is almost hilarious but also not. It's like there's the beginning of a quicksand sucking underfoot and I feel myself wondering for the first time how far this can be pushed, because beyond a certain point, chaos might not be so cool. If it becomes okay for anyone to rob anything, pretty soon no one's safe. After the shops are empty, what's going to be next? Houses? The projects? Kids on the street?

All of them! says Jay. *They're all at it. The feds, the politicians, the bankers—they're all crooks and they just get away with it, so why shouldn't we?*

Suit yourself, says Blaze.

Sort of reluctant but too proud to back off, Jay walks toward Currys. He has to stop for two guys who are carrying a washing machine. *You coming or what?* he says.

I can feel that Karen and Femi want to go with him. They both look at Blaze, but Blaze just walks off down the road. I follow him. Been still so long I got to unsquelch my sneakers from the hot tarmac. After a moment Karen and Femi and Lee are with us. I turn and watch Jay disappear into the swirl of people funneling through the shop door.

Last moment I see him pops out at me like a flash photo, 'cause I get the feeling it's a fork in the road and now his life's going one way, mine another. Don't know why, I just feel it. And turns out I'm right, but not in the way I thought, 'cause it ain't him that's walking off the edge of a cliff, it's me.

There's fires up ahead and everything's getting louder, busier, angrier. We're walking right toward the middle of it all—toward the *boom boom boom* from a corner that's filled with feds wearing helmets and banging their shields—looking like the last stand of some army that knows it's finished.

A building's almost disappeared inside flames that are roaring and snapping out the windows and up the roof—lighting everyone's faces orange. I can feel the heat halfway down the street. The noise of it is a growl you can feel in your chest, and there's also what sounds like a shootout from inside as things crack and shatter and fall. There's fire engines lined up behind the police, but they can't get to it. Feels like it ain't going to be long before the whole thing comes down.

I look at Blaze and he ain't smiling or frowning or nothing. The fire's awesome—a hundred times bigger than any fire I seen before. Huge orange swirls are billowing out and the smoke looks like some kind of dark flood shoving upward into the sky. I always thought smoke wafted and drifted, but this stuff's different; it's thick and heavy and you can see that one lungful would kill you. There's no way anyone left in there is coming out alive.

Everyone knows the whole city burned down once hundreds of years ago, but that always felt like almost a fairy tale till now. Now I can imagine it. This whole building's just gone and it's hard to see what could stop it taking the next one along and the next one after that.

People are chucking bricks and traffic cones and bits of glass and anything they can find toward the feds. There's a Dumpster by the side of the road. Two guys are inside it passing stuff out and it's all getting chucked over the empty strip of road in front of the fire toward the feds. Nobody seems angry. It feels more like a laugh, like the wildest party there's ever been.

Part of me is twitching to run up and throw stuff. We've all been stopped and searched so many times— treated like scum by feds who are just looking for any opportunity to screw us over—and the idea of chucking a brick that might get one of them is beautiful. They get off on reminding us we're nothing. It's obvious in the way they look at us and talk to us and mess us around even when they know we ain't doing nothing bad. So why wouldn't we get off on letting them know they're wrong— letting them know we're here and we ain't nothing and we can fight back? If someone's bullying you and there's nothing you can do to stop them, you dream of hurting them back and of doing all the things you can't in reality. You just do. And now the dream is alive and there's rows of them cowering and there's hundreds of us and we're winning—man, it's one of the sweetest things I ever seen. Concentr8 was just the start. The dam's broke and now everyone's angry about everything—I mean, the anger ain't new; it's letting it out that's new. Don't got words to describe it, 'cause it's vicious and brutal but also innocent like a kid who lets out every feeling without even meaning to.

The whole thing is like heaven and hell rolled into one and I just stand on the spot turning around and around taking it all in—no clue what to think or say or do. All of us have that same look on our face except Blaze. Blaze has a plan.

I soak it up a while longer until Blaze says, *Follow me,* and we all do because you just do when it's Blaze.

We turn down a side street and five minutes further on everything's normal again. You can hear it—you'd have to be deaf not to know total mayhem was everywhere—and you can smell the plasticky smoke that pinches the back of your nose—but where we are now is all quiet and empty and ordinary. The only weird thing is that it's too empty—there's no cars or even people. Here it's almost as if the city's gone to sleep even though the sun's still up. It's kind of eerie—me and Blaze and Karen and Femi and Lee walking down the middle of the street as if we have the whole city to ourselves.

Lee's got a metal rod in his hand—something out of that Dumpster. He goes up to a parked car—a Merc—and smashes the side windows. He tries not to smile, but you can see he enjoys it. Nobody says anything and we just carry on walking. I want a go but I'm too embarrassed to ask.

We don't stop walking till we get to the river, which is just the usual sludgy brown road of cold tea rolling on like normal, like it don't make no difference that everything around it has gone mad. All that water, tons and tons of it always moving, it's amazing when you look close. Even though it's the shittiest water you ever seen, it's still beautiful, just the power of it.

Don't hardly ever come up this far—ain't safe. I'm wondering why Blaze has brought us here until I notice that unlike the rest of us, he ain't looking out at the water. He's facing the other way, looking up at that big glass building where they run the city from—don't even know the name of it, but it's where the mayor works.

Streets ain't so empty around here. There's a few people like us who are out to see what's going on—some others who look like they're going home from work—and even a few people wandering up and down like it's any normal evening and they're off to the cinema or a restaurant or whatever it is people like that do. It's a weird mix with only the muffled wail of a hundred sirens down near our yard giving away what's really going on.

Blaze stares up at that building. He got a look in his eye like an animal that's found its prey.

What's going on? says Femi eventually.

Are you with me or not? says Blaze.

Yeah, says Femi, shrugging like he don't know if Blaze is bullshitting or what.

All the way?

All the way. Ain't convincing the way he says it, but Blaze don't seem to mind.

He turns to me. Fixes me with them icicle eyes. *All the way, Troy?*

I don't know what Blaze is talking about, but it's not like my thoughts even flicker to any other answer. *All the way, man.*

All the way? he says again. This time to Karen.

She don't hesitate, but she don't say nothing either; she just steps forward and kisses him on the mouth deep and long and so hot I actually go a bit hard just watching. Karen's his girlfriend and she's the finest girl in the projects or any other projects in fact. She got blue eyes and dark skin and a single diamond stud the size of a pinhead in her nose and a mouth that's somehow angry and sexy and aloof and cool all at once. She never smiles, but in a weird way it also looks like she's never not smiling. There's a little curl at the edges like she knows something you don't. Nobody has any idea how she paid for the diamond or even if it really is a diamond, but I don't care. If I could kiss that mouth just one time I'd be ready to die.

She don't like me—not as in don't *like* me, but as in actually hates me, but that's another story. It's Blaze who breaks it off and pulls away from her. I don't know how he does, but he does and he turns to Lee.

All the way?

All the way, man, says Lee.

He don't ask us to follow, but when he turns and walks away we all do. He strolls toward the entrance of the glass building, then when a man comes out—a slouchy half-bald bloke with a suit that don't fit right and a gray briefcase—Blaze swerves and changes course. We go with him and now it seems like we're all following this guy.

When we're around the corner—in a narrow street that leads to the main road—Blaze calls out to him. *WHERE YOU GOING?*

The guy stops and turns. You can see the whole calculation on his face. Run away or talk my way out of it? Play it cool or spring before it gets any worse? He knows we're bad news and he's right. It takes him less than half a second to realize that whatever it is we got in mind for him can't be run away from. Not a lardy old guy like him up against us—he wouldn't get more than a few steps.

Home, he says almost casual but with a crack in his voice that shows he's shitting bricks.

You work for the mayor? says Blaze.

Another telltale pause. More cogs whirring in the guy's head. *No.*

We saw you coming out. You're wearing an ID badge.

Like an idiot the guy pulls the ID badge off and hides it in his pocket. *I'm in the housing department. I've got nothing to do with the mayor. I've never even met him.*

I didn't say you had, says Blaze.

Lee slaps his metal bar into the palm of his hand.

What do you want? he says. *You want my phone? Take it. Have it.*

He hands his phone to Blaze. Blaze takes it, glances at it, drops it on the floor, and stands on it. There's a little scrape and a crack as it crushes under his twisting heel. *I don't want your shit phone.*

Karen and Lee crack up. The guy's eyes are flicking everywhere—he knows he's trapped.

What do you want?

Blaze stares at him not speaking. He sucks his teeth, making a sinister wet squeak like a mouse being strangled. *That's what I'm trying to decide,* says Blaze, but you can tell he's only messing with the guy, drawing out his terror.

Well, I wish I could stay and help out, but I really have to get home.

The guy turns and tries to walk away, but he don't get more than one step before Blaze grabs him from behind with an arm around the neck. The muscles on Blaze's arms stand out like the twists in a rope. He ain't much older than me, but he got the body of a man already with a thick fuzz on his top lip, and he's taller than the guy by a head at least.

I think what I want is for you to listen. You and everyone else. Blaze's voice is quiet and deep and slow like always. He never shouts, but now there's steel in it.

The guy's face is ketchup red. It don't look like he can breathe. If this was a cartoon there'd be smoke coming out his ears. After a while Blaze slackens his hold and he coughs air back into his lungs.

I'm listening! says the guy eventually. *I'm listening!*

That ain't what I got in mind, says Blaze, and at the same moment the briefcase falls onto the tarmac. It don't even look like he dropped it on purpose. Something in him has given up and his muscles have gone limp.

Can you feel this? says Blaze.

Yes! says the man, almost shrieking it. His eyes are rolling in their sockets with red jags popping up like he's stoned but it ain't that, it's something else completely. I don't know what the two of them's talking about.

Can you feel THIS?

The guy yelps and his torso jolts—twisting, lurching, but not getting out of Blaze's grip. Now he's moved, I see that Blaze has a shank pressed into his back.

I glance up. Lee's licking his lips, nervous, afraid, looking same as me, like he had no idea this was going to happen. Karen's eyes are wide too and she's half smiling, but I have no idea what that means. Femi's got a face like he just pissed himself. I don't reckon anyone was in on this.

Careful, I say. *There's cameras.*

Blaze looks up scanning for CCTV, and there's a moment when it's like we're dreaming or floating, 'cause time just does this hover—I swear, it feels as if the whole city's gone quiet waiting for Blaze to decide what to do next.

It's Karen who ends it, snapping, *Get him! Just get him!* She's got the weirdest look in her eye, like she forgot everything, just gone off the edge wild and animal. It's like everything's been stripped away and just for a flash this is the real her— the pure, naked Karen, and I swear it's vicious.

But all this, everything that's happened up to now, it ain't nothing—ain't even half a step away from normal life compared to what happens next. Takes us all a minute to even understand what he means when Blaze finally speaks up, 'cause what he's saying takes everything to a new level. He don't say it loud—don't say it like it's even anything special—but everyone hears and it's so crazy nobody speaks up or tries to stop him. We all just go along with it.

You're coming with us, he says.

Hyperactivity…was first recognised in the mid-nineteenth century by German physician Heinrich Hoffman, who in 1844 wrote a popular collection of nursery rhymes entitled *Der Struwwelpeter*…One of his creations was Fidgety Philip, who causes chaos at the dinner table.

Matthew Smith, *Hyperactive: The Controversial History of ADHD*

FEMI

One minute it's a laugh just scaring the guy, nothing bad, nothing actually mental, then next thing you know he's pulled a shank and we're dragging the guy off and I'm thinking, *NO ONE ASKED ME!?* I'm thinking, *I'M NOT INTO THIS WHAT YOU DOING THIS IS CRAZY BAD*, but I mean, it was too late by then, wasn't it?

That's Blaze, though. I swear, it's lethal being around him 'cause you don't know what you're going to be dragged into, and Mum always says, *Stay away, stay away from that Blaze*, and I know she's right, but it ain't that easy, is it? It's like a magnetic force, you get pulled in, don't know how, you just do.

I could've walked off. Right then. But nobody said this is your last chance. Nobody said this is your last second to choose to be normal—to go to school and do stuff and be an ordinary person.

He should have told us. Asked us. I mean, this wasn't no small thing, this was big-time, but Blaze don't do that. He don't give you no choice. I mean, he asked me if I was in and maybe I did say yes, but it's not like he said what I was in *for*, 'cause if I'd known, it would have been, *NO WAY!* It would have been, *NO WAY YOU'RE CRACKED MAN!* And that would have been it. I would have been out of there.

So next thing we're walking with the guy to the bus stop, I mean—the BUS STOP!? You can't kidnap someone on a bus, that's just stupid, but I mean, the shank's right there and he knows it, so he can't do nothing. You can see from his face that he thinks he's two seconds away from death, just one false step and Blaze'll stab him, and I don't reckon he would. I mean, Blaze is bad, but not that bad. He's too clever. Wouldn't stab nobody out in the open, I mean, that's basically suicide, ain't it? But the guy, he don't know that.

Shank's in Blaze's pocket and we're all around the guy all the way to the bus stop. Can't get over it, man; I mean, if that was the plan it's insane, but the guy's like all limp and he knows he can't run away, so what can he do?

You can see him pleading with his eyes, staring at people walking past, just begging them to help him, but nobody's looking, and even if they were, they wouldn't care or wouldn't step in, 'cause nobody wants to mess with our sort. Ain't worth it. Everyone knows that, even if you only been in the city five minutes.

Bus comes and we get on. All of us. I swear, it's the maddest thing.

I could've run off then. Easy. Could've just not got on the bus, walked away, whatever. I mean, that's what I should've done, I ain't stupid. But it's hard to describe that feeling, it's like you're on rails or something, 'cause it was all of us, it wasn't like I was thinking for just me. We were a unit and I mean, I wasn't in control, I was only a passenger. Blaze had it all laid out in advance, or he seemed to anyway, and when he's decided what's going to happen, that's what happens. Ain't nothing you can do to stop it. I didn't have the power to change anything. I swear, he can make you do stuff you couldn't even think of, wouldn't do in a million years if it was just you on your own.

Sometimes I feel almost like the buzz for him ain't that he even wants to do it—whatever it is—it's that he wants to see how far he can push us. Wants to feel what he can make other people do. And the more we're doing what we don't like, the more he's feeling his power, swimming in it, just basking in how he's got us where he wants us.

Mum was right with that *Stay away from Blaze*, she was more right than she ever could've known.

Blaze and Troy have something dead in them, something cold that won't never be warmed up by nothing. Can't even imagine them ever living in a normal apartment, having a normal job, just being normal. I'm different, I ain't like that. Shouldn't have got mixed up with them, 'cause I ain't got the stomach for that life, ain't got the balls. And I ain't got the smarts to bail out when I ought to, neither.

Didn't even know where that bus was taking us. Should've asked. Should've just got out and walked home. Wouldn't have even had to say anything, not a word. Could've just walked. Been over it hundreds of times in my head and that's the craziest thing—all them minutes ticking by slow as you like, and me just sitting there on that bus letting Blaze take me off into his madness—take me out of the life I had up to that day, into some other place that wasn't never meant for a kid like me.

I don't even got the excuse that it happened too fast— that I didn't have time to think about what I was doing— 'cause I did. I had all that time on the bus and I didn't do nothing with it, so I suppose you could say I deserve everything that happened to me.

So eventually we get out of the bus and we gone miles. It's Hackney or something, I don't know. The bus empties everyone out before the high street, because apparently things are kicking off around here too. Blaze acts like he knows where we are, and leads on without looking worried or confused or nothing. He don't let the guy farther away than the length of his arm. Just stays ready to grab him at any moment. Or stab him. Whatever.

The guy stumbles around like some zombie, his skin weird and tight around his eyes and his neck so rigid it's like his spine has turned to metal. His face goes white then red when Blaze drags him over to a cash machine. Don't know when it happened, but looks like Blaze's already got his wallet. Asks the guy for his PIN and he just starts begging, *Please don't do this, please,* then stupid shit like, *I'll give it to you if you let me go. Will you let me go when I tell you?* But Blaze don't even respond and eventually he gives the number.

Types it in. Nothing.

You can see the guy's eyes spiraling everywhere, trying to think of a way out, trying to think of how he can run for it, but he can't, there's no way. We got him. There's people around and he could just scream and lash out, but he knows that would be a risk, a big risk with the shank so close and Blaze so cold. He's working on it, though, trying to calculate his options, then you can see his head goes limp and drops when he decides it ain't worth it, and all slow like his mouth is filled with sand or something, the four numbers come out.

Types them in. Hundred quid. Just like that. The five neatest, flattest bills you ever seen.

Pulls out the card and pushes it right back in. Types in them magic numbers. Hundred more! Man, it's so crazy; we ain't never done nothing like this, and worse than ever

I just want to get out, but there's a pull now 'cause I got to see what we do with all that money. I mean, it's ours now, a whole fat stack of it to do whatever we want.

Blaze puts the numbers in again, but this time no dice. It's maxed out at two hundred and none of us ever seen that much cash in one place. It's like wings, I swear; lifts us up and carries us down the street.

Blaze gives twenty to Troy to go get some fries and stuff, then gives me twenty and don't say nothing, just points to a candy shop.

Walk in and start piling stuff up on the counter and the guy watches me every second, don't move his eyes off me for a moment, and there's chocolate and sweets and chips and everything, and when I hand over that crisp, perfect twenty you can see for a moment he don't even want to take it. He knows it ain't really mine. But ain't no difference between me and him, because he takes it right enough. Rings up the stuff and it's sixteen something, so I keep piling on more until it's right up to £19.73.

He bags it and passes me the change real slow and reluctant, like he's too good to do nothing for a little shit like me. Holds it out with his arm half bent so I got to reach out to take it. I let it hang there, don't take the money and tell him to put it in the charity so he knows I ain't cheap. I wait and watch till he puts it in, like I think he might steal it, so he knows what it feels like, 'cause that's what he's been thinking of me all along.

By the time I'm back Troy's got two bags of food, Blaze has got bottles of White Ace and WKD, and I've got the snacks, so we're well set up for a big night. Don't let the guy go, though. I mean, I would if it was up to me. What more do we want from him? But Blaze got other plans and he leads us off away from the sound of sirens and fighting and down weird roads where there ain't even apartment buildings or nothing, just fences and garages and warehouses. Then we come to some train tracks and there's a gap in the wire and without even asking if we're up for it he leads us on and over the tracks. And that man is still with us like some puppet at the end of Blaze's arm.

Troy gives me a weird look as we go over the tracks. Like he knows something. Not afraid exactly, but kind of resigned. I get a little acid jolt up the back of my throat when I turn back from the other side and see the gap in the fence and think to myself, What if I never get back there? What if this is a one-way trip?

I already know I messed up worse than I ever messed up before, but I keep on going, don't I? Just follow the others without even thinking for myself and I don't reckon I'll ever be able to explain why.

World's full of mysteries, ain't it? Who made the Earth and the animals and what happens after we're dead and all that shit, but the biggest mystery of all is why we do what we do. It's the one thing we ought to know better than anything else, but sometimes you just don't.

Charles Bradley (1902–1979)...prescribed the amphetamine Benzedrine to his patients in an effort to stimulate the replacement of spinal fluid and relieve the children's headaches. The drug did little for the headaches, but teachers at Bradley Home observed that it seemed to improve the ability of patients to learn and behave at school. After testing the drug further, Bradley began using it regularly...By 1950 he had used it on 275 children and found that it was effective over 60 per cent of the time.

Matthew Smith, *Hyperactive: The Controversial History of ADHD*

KAREN

It's the weirdest place I ever been? Over the tracks and over this wall and then through a tiny gap in these massive folding doors, and by the time we go in it's getting dark and you can't hardly see nothing inside. No proper lights or nothing, but Troy and Femi rig up some pissy little lamps like you get on a desk or something and that just makes it worse? Just shadows everywhere? This huge room like a factory or something but empty and dusty and wrecked, just full of abandoned shit nobody even wants. Concrete floor and miles of empty metal racks and tires and bits of cars and small high-up windows made of wrinkly glass that don't even let in no light. The lamps are too bright to look at—they just make this little pool we got to sit in— and behind us and above us there's these huge shadows dancing when we move, so spooky it makes your blood cold, I swear.

Me and Blaze go into a little room where you can't hardly see nothing. He tells me to watch the guy and he takes out his shank, and my heart starts going crazy fast 'cause I don't want that. I mean, that's just evil, but he puts it in his mouth and climbs up to a window where there's a big slatty blind? Takes the shank out his mouth and cuts the cord. There's a massive *SSSHHHHHHHHHHHHHK* as the blind slices down, makes my whole body shudder so hard I nearly lift off the ground, 'cause it's like the sound of an ax or something. The guy's eyes are almost popping out his head now, he's just so losing it.

Blaze tests the cord and it looks thin but strong. He gets another one from the next window and shoves the guy down next to a radiator and ties him up. They don't say nothing. Neither of them. I just want to get out of there, 'cause I don't know what's going on now, I'm kind of freaking?

Back in the big room they're all sitting on the floor eating and me and Blaze get some and then we're drinking and it ain't long before we almost forget there's a guy tied up next door.

We done all-nighters in weird places before. Just around on night buses or in parks. I mean, it's a laugh. Ain't scary or nothing 'cause it's us everyone's scared of. I swear, wherever we go, if it's late enough people just run off, leave us to it? But this is different and maybe that's why we just stay up, 'cause sleeping here, that's too weird.

Don't nobody know the way back except Blaze, so there ain't no option of bailing and anyway, once we all been drinking and Blaze has put on some music from his phone and we got some food inside us, I don't reckon anyone wants to go anyway, 'cause the feeling that's making us scared flips over, and on the other side there's this kind of crazy laughing dancing shouting not caring about nothing vibe that sort of wipes out all the spookiness and makes it feel like a party, like the most secret, exclusive, weirdest party you've ever been invited to, like this ain't never going to be repeated and it's almost magic that you got to be there. Like years later people's going to be saying, *D'you hear about that amazing night when blah blah blah* and you's the one's going to be able to stand up and say, *Yeah—I was there.*

I mean, the days can all just end up being the same, can't they? Monday, Tuesday, Wednesday, on and on, always the same. Then there's something like this and it's like, *BOOM!* So why would you walk away? From that? 'Cause now minute to minute we don't know nothing about what's going to happen next, and walking away, I mean, that's like saying you'd rather be dead than alive, ain't it? Maybe you'd've done different, but maybe you wouldn't, 'cause you can't know till you're in it.

No idea what time it is, but eventually when there's nothing left to drink and it's proper late everyone just flattens some boxes to put over the concrete and flops out. Blaze whispers he's got a place for us and he leads me by the hand to this rusty metal staircase in the corner, takes us up to like a balcony or something? Looks down over the whole place? And off the balcony there's like an office, and we go in, and it ain't half so wrecked as everywhere else, and there's even a sofa and Blaze lifts me—lifts me like I don't weigh nothing—and sits me on the desk and I'm about to say that I'm freaking that this is just too weird but then he's got his arms around me and I'm folded into him and he's kissing my neck and half the words don't even come out of my mouth right, 'cause I don't know, it's like I'm melting. My whole body just melting into him 'cause he's just raw and strong and when he wants you, there ain't nothing you can do to stop yourself giving in to the power of it. Nothing.

Day Two

Ritalin was first synthesized in 1944 by CIBA scientist Leandro Panizzon. Panizzon's wife, Marguerite, whose nickname was Rita, used the drug prior to playing tennis on account of her low blood pressure, and Panizzon named the stimulant after her.

Matthew Smith, *Hyperactive: The Controversial History of ADHD*

THE MAYOR

I'm a handsome bugger. No, I am. Ask anyone, as long as they're female. Gents don't see it. They sense the aura, but they can't tell where it comes from.

Okay, so maybe *handsome* isn't the word. I'm perfectly willing to concede that there's a hint of potato about the shape of my head. It's a trifle too large, a shade chin-heavy, lacking in bone structure, not what you'd call conventionally good-looking. In America I wouldn't stand a chance, not in politics, but we Brits are better than that.

Women have always been drawn to me. I am a talented seducer. Hence politics. For what is politics but seduction on a national scale? As some wit once wrote, "Hugo Nelson knows how to find the clitoris of the Tory Party." I couldn't have put it better myself.

I've never been much good at sports. Chasing around after inflated sacks of leather hasn't ever struck me as a particularly dignified or fruitful pursuit. A man's pride, however, often pivots on such abilities, especially when young. Everyone wants to be an alpha male. Everyone worth knowing, anyway. If kicking and throwing isn't your thing, the only other path up that all-important Greek alphabet is bedroom prowess. By which I don't mean performance. I simply mean that the woman you have on your arm tells the other men in the room where you rank. The more they want your woman, the more they respect you.

Of course, this is all strictly *entre nous*. A politician can never say such things aloud. The feminist harpies would crush you, roast you over a hot flame, and serve you up with whole wheat quinoa on the food pages of the *Guardian*. You can't get anywhere these days unless you've mastered the art of keeping a straight face while you pay lip service to every pseudo-oppressed, whining, scrounging, blood-sucking minority there is. Not that women are a minority, by the way, but you know what I mean. Even when you've got a true blue Tory heart, you have to have the tongue of a Commie these days if you don't want to be slaughtered in the press. That's just how things are.

Which brings me to the point. Journalists. Bloody journalists. One arriving any minute. Hence me looking in the mirror, straightening tie, checking coiffure, admiring own handsomeness.

It's this hair that's the key. Hollywood blond. You have to be memorable. The hair is my magic touch. Faced with a crowd of gray-suited old farts, I'm the only one anyone can remember. If the curse of baldness had struck, I wouldn't be standing where I am today. I'd be one of the minions slaving away in those airless offices down below. Hard to imagine. I wouldn't be me, frankly. I certainly wouldn't be running the greatest city in the world. Substance is crucial, of course—brains, application, ruthlessness, oratory, insight, ambition, etc., etc.—but you can't underestimate the importance of good follicles. Every ballot box in the world is crying out for a sprinkling of glamour, and in politics just not looking like a lump of dim sum counts as catwalk chic. The bar is pretty low, let's face it, on the looks front.

The intercom buzzes. It's Andrea, telling me the journo is here. Good girl, Andrea. Not the sharpest tool in the box, but shapely, biddable, and eminently discreet.

I check my hair one last time, admire the view for a minute or two so the journalist feels as if he has been kept waiting, then sit at my desk in front of an official-looking document (checking first that it's nothing iffy—these bastards can read upside down and they have no morals).

"Come," I say, relishing the feel of the imperative verbal form emanating from my mouth. At home, nobody listens to a word I say. The era of domestic obedience is long gone, like an archaeological stratum lost underfoot, barely even remembered. It is therefore absolutely vital to a man's ego that he has a job where he possesses employees who obey. The workplace is the only remaining space where a man can feel like a man. How other chaps cope with being a minion at home and then a minion at work is quite beyond me. It must devour the soul.

The journalist walks in. I hadn't even checked the name. I was expecting the usual nicotine-fingered, slouching, chippy bloke with no tie and unpolished shoes—redbrick degree and a hard-on for scoring points over anyone with a hint of Oxbridge in their demeanor—you know the type. I certainly wasn't expecting this: a female, young, pert, and exquisitely assembled. Quite mouth-watering, like a bowl of ice cream waiting for a spoon. She's got that ball-breaking look, with button-it-in-but-show-it-off clothes, bloodred lips, and a hundred-and-fifty-quid haircut, but I'm the kind of man who likes a challenge. Not wife material, of course, hard work over the long haul, but someone you certainly wouldn't walk past at a cocktail party without at least testing the waters.

The first tool of seduction is the emission of an erotic signal akin to sonar. Not explicitly audible, it can be sent off in all directions without disturbing anyone, since it only bounces back off objects that merit a place on the radar screen. Few things in life are more exciting than that first *blip* of response.

I walk around the desk to shake her hand. Eyeball to eyeball, I give her the charisma special. The full Bill Clinton.

Methylphenidate's [Ritalin's] effects are rather similar to those of amphetamine, which was widely used in the 1960s as a stimulant. It is an interesting reflection on the change in attitude to psychoactive drugs over time that back then amphetamine was widely known as 'speed', and viewed with suspicion, rather as Ecstasy is now.

Steven Rose, *The 21st Century Brain*

THE JOURNALIST

I've seen it a thousand times before. That look. Bored, lecherous old man perking up at the sight of a pair of tits. Not that there's anything to see. I know his reputation, so I'm buttoned up right to the neck, but that isn't enough. You have to wear a sack on your head to stop guys like this giving you the eye.

"I don't believe we've met before," he says.

"I'm features. Not politics."

"Of course. Of course. This is a profile piece, isn't it? Do sit. Coffee?"

"Black. No sugar." (I actually prefer it milky, but I've found that ordering black coffee makes people take you more seriously. It's often the first question you're asked, and it helps to give the impression of gravitas. You don't actually have to drink it.)

He gestures me toward a sofa in the corner of his office while an underling retreats with our order. Out of his window, there's a panorama across the Thames that's one of the best views of London I've ever seen. Centuries of history and billions of pounds of real estate all visible in a single sweep—from horizon to horizon, one unimaginably complex knot of human endeavor. There can be few other spots on the planet to match it. From up here, the city looks as diligent and industrious as ever—strangely, serenely normal—as if nothing has happened.

It occurs to me that it would be possible for a man working from this office to have no clue about what has taken over the streets. Only a few wisps of smoke, drifting up from the east, give any hint of the chaos. His view is dominated by the tower blocks of the Square Mile, teetering stacks of bankers, millionaire perched upon millionaire.

The mayor sits in an armchair opposite me, a chair that is, of course, a couple of inches higher than the sofa.

"Not so much a profile as a kind of how-did-we-get-here piece," I say.

"And the photographer?" he asks, one hand rising to caress his fringe.

"He's coming later."

"Of course."

"So," I say, placing my digital recorder on the coffee table between us, "how did we get here?"

He laughs nervously, a high, effeminate bark that seems to take us both by surprise. "That's very direct. Aren't you going to soften me up with some easy questions first?"

This is his version of charm, which seems to circle the outer suburbs of flirtation. The attempt is a little halfhearted, as if he knows this isn't going to work, but it's almost a reflex. He can't switch it off.

"Would you like me to?" I say, a gratifyingly subtle put-down.

"No, no. Of course not. So—how did we get here? Well... the situation is very grave...and...er...obviously the police are doing everything they can to restore law and order in highly challenging circumstances. Were my people given all the details about this interview? I honestly thought it was just a profile. Not too political. Aren't you from a magazine?"

"A weekend supplement. Are you uncomfortable discussing politics?"

"Of course not. It's just that I'm giving daily press conferences, and this is a time when obviously there's a huge amount for me to be doing…"

It's clear that I need to change tack. Spikiness isn't working.

I shift my position on the sofa, leaning toward him as if he is a rare and fascinating specimen I can't quite believe my luck to have encountered in the flesh. It's easy to forget, interviewing a man like the mayor, that you have to use the same techniques as on any fragile-egoed actor or musician. If you forget to act as if they are mesmerizing creatures who are displaying extraordinary generosity in bestowing their time on a mere journalist, you've lost them.

"Your people wanted a chance to get across the background," I say, my voice lower, warmer, breathier. "The stuff that gets left behind in the cut and thrust of press conferences. The idea was to give people a chance to see the real you—a sense of how a personality like yours copes under the strain of demanding circumstances."

I'm now perched on the edge of the sofa, pen poised over a blank page of my notebook, my eyes brimming with expectation and enthrallment. I might be overdoing it.

"Your side of the story," I add. "The man behind the mask. That kind of thing."

"Of course. Quite right. Yes. Naturally, I…well, let's go back to the beginning. I mean…in policy terms, since the last riots, we have scored some great successes. This is what's getting overlooked. We took some great strides forward, thanks to the policies I implemented, but now we are facing a setback. A major setback."

"Great strides forward? Are you referring to your policy on Concentr8?"

"Absolutely. The introduction of Concentr8 was an unqualified success for several years. Schools were behind it, parents were behind it, the medical profession was behind it, the police were behind it."

"But wasn't the Concentr8 policy designed to prevent something like this happening again?"

"I employed Professor Pyle after the last riots to look carefully into the issue of youth mental health, and with the benefit of his vast expertise, he recommended to me a decisive and effective solution. The medical profession has made huge progress in treating disorders that create disruptive behavior in schools and in many cases criminal behavior outside the school grounds. The police know who these people are, teachers know who they are, and guiding them away from the kind of misbehavior in school that leads so often to petty crime and then serious crime, with a straightforward diagnosis and a tried-and-tested cure, is doing a great service both to them and to society."

"But Concentr8 is a new drug."

"Professor Pyle is a highly respected figure in the world of mental health. Concentr8 was his recommendation, on the grounds that it has fewer side effects, is significantly cheaper, and is in every way an improvement on other ADHD medications. Support for the program, from the start, was enormous. The effect on school results and truancy was immediately noticeable."

The coffee underling, who has entered the office without making a sound, places our drinks between us. I take a sip of the bitter fluid and ask, "Is it the job of a mayor to prescribe medicine?"

"Of course not. But when society is suffering from a disease, it is my job to diagnose what's wrong with this city and to seek a cure. My policy was simply to take a more proactive role in helping troubled children receive medical help. Prevention rather than punishment. It was a visionary policy that to the dismay of my detractors was an immediate success."

"At that point, before the current difficulties, there was some talk of you as a rival to the party leader. There were whispers of you leaving the mayor's office to stand for prime minister. Was there any truth in that?"

The mayor lets out a short cackle, which is probably intended to sound self-deprecating, but the effect doesn't quite come off. "The...er...the prime minister has always had my full backing."

"But you blame him for the current situation."

"It's not a question of blame. The economic climate is a challenging one, and cuts had to be made. It's true that I urged him not to withdraw funding for the Concentr8 program, and we had very robust debates on this matter, but...I suppose I simply...without wanting to give any impression of a split within the party...I feel it's important for Londoners to know that events on the streets today are not a result of the introduction of Concentr8. It's the withdrawal of Concentr8 that has led to the current crisis, and I can't pretend this is a cut that ever had my approval."

"So you do blame the prime minister."

"Of course not. At times like this, difficult choices have to be made."

"Do you have any comment on the rumors of an abduction from outside your office?"

"I never comment on rumors. Police are examining some CCTV footage, and there will be an announcement if the situation evolves."

"One last question…"

"Do you really have everything you need? I thought you wanted the man behind the mask."

"Your PA said I was only allowed ten minutes."

"Did he?"

"Apparently you have a meeting with some kind of emergency task force."

"I suppose I do."

"I just wanted to ask if you have any message for the rioters."

"Just to…well, to stop it. At once. Enough is enough. Things have got out of hand and they need to know they will be punished. The rule of law will prevail. We will give no quarter to unbridled thuggery."

"And is there a question of dependency? Some people are suggesting that the removal of Concentr8 might be causing withdrawal symptoms en masse. Could this be a factor in the riots?"

"There is no question of Concentr8 being an addictive substance. Absolutely not. You'll have to ask Professor Pyle about this. He's the doctor. Rigorous procedures are in place for testing everything that is prescribed in this country. Concentr8 is one hundred percent safe."

"Would you give it to your children?"

"My children are in rude health. Literally. Thank you for your time. It's been a pleasure."

The mayor stands, shakes my hand briskly, strides to his desk, and stares at his computer screen with a now-I-want-it-to-look-as-if-I-am-hard-at-work expression settling over his face.

The interview is over. I get the feeling I haven't made it onto Hugo Nelson's Christmas card list.

FEMI

It's strong, that White Ace. Next morning my head's exploding, that's if it is morning. Don't feel like it, 'cause it's already proper hot—sun slanting in, pushing gray-orange rays through the high windows so dirty they ain't hardly windows at all.

It's the first look I've got of where we ended up. Can't even tell if it's a factory or a warehouse or what. Bigger than a soccer field, with racks along one whole wall, mostly empty except for a few car parts and tools. Massive heap of old worn tires in the corner, half toppled over like spilled guts. Gray machines along one wall, big old rusty things for doing I don't know what, and more tools covered in greasy dust almost like fur. There's struts and pipes and cables and wires all across the ceiling, probably just like any other building, except in a place like this, you don't bother to hide them. Floor's concrete, all smooth and polished and warm if you rub through the dirt. Crunches underfoot, though, with every kind of filth you can think of. Don't know why, but lots of feathers. Gray ones.

Smells like you'd expect. Dust and oil and maybe some animal rotting somewhere what we ain't found yet. There's something moldy, sort of musty, you can taste in the back of your mouth, which is weird with everything so hot and dry and baked.

The others are all asleep when I wake—Blaze and Karen up in the office, Troy and Lee down with me on boxes. When I look over I see Troy's dead still, but his eyes are open. There's something about Troy makes you wonder if he ever sleeps; he just ain't the kind of person you can imagine switched off. Dad told me once they used to take a canary in a cage down into coal mines so if there was bad air the canary would snuff it and the miners would know they had to get out. That's Troy. He's our canary. Small and always worried, and if anything bad happens, you always reckon it'll be Troy that takes the hit.

There ain't no sound from where the guy's tied up, but I swear I can feel waves of him coming out of that room. I mean, what if he's dead? It's stupid, but he could be. Heart attack or something, I mean, he looked on the verge, he really did.

Can't think of nothing to say to Troy. That's the stupid thing. I want to know if he's part of the plan. If he knew what was going to happen. Or if he can help me out. I mean, maybe we could just run for it, 'cause I swear it ain't just the White Ace that's made my skull buzz and scream like this. Sick, I just feel sick in my head and my stomach and my bones and every part of me, 'cause I know I got in too deep, into something that ain't part of my world.

Troy? I say.

He turns and looks at me but don't say nothing.

You okay? I ask.

He shrugs. What kind of answer's that? I mean, this is the weirdest thing that's ever happened and he's acting like it's normal! But him and Blaze, they're almost psychic. Whatever you say to Troy you might as well say it straight to Blaze, 'cause there ain't no gap between them.

I lean in and whisper. Don't know why. I mean, it's only Lee there, and he's asleep, and even when he's awake it ain't like that adds much to the number of working brain cells.

You into this? I say.

Troy licks his lips. I can see he's stressing over his answer 'cause he'd never say nothing against Blaze, but I can feel that he knows this is too heavy.

Dunno, he says.

Didn't hear him coming or nothing, don't know how he does it, but I turn and do this massive flinch 'cause suddenly Blaze is right there standing over us, wearing no top, and he's ripped and he's half smiling down at me like he knows what I just said. Knows it so well he don't even need to ask.

All right, man? he asks, but not even looking at me. Just stepping past and getting a box of what's left of the fries. Tips on more ketchup and eats them cold.

My heart's pumping and pumping; it's like I can feel each pulse pushing out at my temples—*doof, doof, doof*—'cause I know what I want to say but I'm scared. Staying here and being part of this is suicide, total suicide, so however hard it is to face down Blaze, it's worse to just play along and do nothing and wait for the feds. So eventually I force it out, trying to say it all casual, but it don't come out like that 'cause my voice is thin and dry and you can hear everything I'm thinking in just the way the words sound.

Might go home, I say.

Blaze stops chewing. Looks at me. Sucks a bit of stuck food from behind his front teeth. Chews some more. Swallows. Sniffs.

I don't reckon that's a good idea, he says.

My mum. She'll be losing it. Don't want to, but I got to.

Lee's awake now, looking from me to Blaze and back again 'cause even he can feel the tension, even he knows something's up.

Blaze shakes his head. *Don't got to do nothing. It's your life.*

I shrug. *Sorry, man.*

Still ain't walking away, though. He's got me pinned down with his eyes. *Well, I ain't going to stop you, but if you go off, then how do I know you won't rat us out?*

I wouldn't do that! You crazy!? I stand up, but my legs don't feel right.

I'm just saying. You should stay. I reckon you'd be safer here.

It's that word safer that gets me. It's all he needs to say. I got no idea how he'd do what he's saying he'd do, or even exactly what it is, but there ain't no doubt that's a threat. He puts a hand on my shoulder and pushes me down into a chair.

Have these, he says, and gives me the rest of the fries. Only the small ones left.

There's a bang from up high—a door slamming. It's Karen coming out of the office. She don't look down, does this big stretch, and she's in underwear and a vest top, and me and Lee and Troy and Blaze all look up at her, totally silent, just frozen. All of us thinking the same thing except maybe Blaze, 'cause for him it don't take no imagination.

It's only 'cause of the silence while we look up at Karen that we hear the noise. Tiny it is. Like a sob. Maybe a gasp. Coming from the guy in the next room.

Anyone fed him? says Blaze.

As American politicians, educators and scientists began analysing why they were falling behind the Soviets, they came to identify and subsequently demonize the behaviours seen to interfere with high educational achievement...A new educational profession, school counsellors, worked with teachers to identify hyperactive children who were struggling academically, label their deficiencies and refer them to physicians for diagnosis and treatment. Through this function, counsellors served as the lynchpin between the educational and medical spheres in the diagnosing of hyperactivity, ensuring that what was initially an educational problem became a medical issue as well.

Matthew Smith, *Hyperactive: The Controversial History of ADHD*

THE HOSTAGE

The sun is coming through a high pane of eight small, dirty windows, one of which is broken, producing seven dull columns and one luminous shaft of sunlight. Dust motes rise casually through the glare in an endless upward flow. At the brightest point they glitter and twinkle. This is the only movement in the room, apart from the steady but imperceptible creep of the sunbeam, which since dawn has moved halfway from the wall to the radiator where I'm tied. In the same time again it will spear down directly onto my head, like the annunciation, except not.

I sometimes hear trains: the clickety-clack of long InterCitys, not the rumble and thump of a Tube line. I'm probably somewhere near the tracks out of Liverpool Street, but that doesn't tell me much. I can't remember the last time

I didn't know where I was. It's like a form of sensory deprivation, to have no idea of your own location. But that's hardly my biggest anxiety.

I don't know how I got through the night. Just making it to the first glimmer of sunrise feels like the hardest thing I've ever done. Not that I actually did anything, but never before have I understood that simply waiting could be so arduous—every hour like the last mile of a marathon.

There isn't enough slack in the cord to lie down. I tried to cut through it by rubbing against the side of the radiator, but all I achieved was removing a layer of skin. The pain in my wrists comes and goes. I keep checking my fingers, worrying that they're swelling up, losing circulation. They tingle and feel puffy, taut, sausagey, but I don't know what that means. My arms and back take turns competing in the pain league. Shifts in posture succeed only in shuffling the pack of aches.

I feel curiously detached from gnawing hunger pangs that seem both intense and distant. Thirst is stronger. My raw and parched throat is impossible to ignore.

And like a pounding mental heartbeat thumping again and again at the inside of my skull, two thoughts beat out an incessant rhythm.

What are they going to do to me?

What do they want?

What are they going to do to me?

What do they want?

What are they going to do to me?

What do they want?

The cold, leaden gaze of the kid with the cornrows, the one in charge, has branded itself into my brain. I am at the mercy of a boy who feels no fear, who has no conscience. He can do anything he likes to me.

I feel his arm around my neck again, hard as steel cable—the sensation absolutely vivid—then, as if zapped by a cattle prod, my body jolts awake.

I don't know how many times I've been through this cycle, or for how long I drift off. All I know is that sickening jab as I crash into alertness, flipping from a dream of strangulation into a reality that is almost as hideous.

I sense a vibration in my throat, a moan that I don't even choose to utter, and barely hear.

I watch the dust motes floating upward.

I should try to imagine myself as one of those weightless fragments of dirt.

Somewhere else in the room, in darkness, the dust must fall back to earth. It must circuit around and around.

I have to detach myself from my body. I have to stop thinking.

I am a speck of dust.

This pain is not mine.

That pain is not mine, those wrists are not mine, those fingers are not mine.

I am a speck of dust.

I rise. I sparkle for a moment. I fall.

There is a sharp squeak as the door scrapes open. I sit up straight, like a schoolboy wanting to look diligent at the arrival of a teacher.

It's the kid in a green T-shirt, the one who pointed out the CCTV cameras and stopped the other one stabbing me. He's the one I'm least afraid of.

I tell myself to be sane, to be normal, to haul my brain back from its long, strange plummet. I am not a speck of dust. I am a man tied to a radiator. I am Anthony Paxton. I work in the housing department at the mayor's office. I live in a room near Finsbury Park. My room is still there, but at this moment is vacant, because I have been kidnapped. By kids.

He puts a cardboard tray of chicken and fries in front of me and unties one hand. It's the first food I've had since yesterday's lunch. The fries are decent, but the chicken is barely even chicken: cold, deep fried, leathery gray, in batter that tastes like a cross between grilled cheddar and orange soda.

I'm so hungry I wolf down the whole lot and gnaw the last strands of meat off the bone, smearing my cheeks with grease in the process. He stands there, watching me eat, as if he's surprised that I'm hungry, as if he's forgotten, until now, that I'm a human being.

"Can I have a drink?" I say. My tongue feels sluggish, fat, unfamiliar.

He takes a moment to respond. I sense that he doesn't want to help me, doesn't want to fetch and carry things for me like a servant, but that he also doesn't want to be responsible for killing me.

He walks out with no indication of whether or not he's going to return, but after a while he does, carrying a large plastic bottle, full, wet on the outside as if it's just been filled at a tap. I gulp heavily from the slightly sweet, alcohol-fragranced water. The liquid seems to tip not just into my stomach, but to seep instantly everywhere, moistening the whole of my parched body.

When I finish, and look up at him, his eyes flit away.

"What's your name?" I say.

I want him to talk, want him to stay. I've been alone for so long I feel like I need to speak to someone, hear another voice, just to check that I haven't lost my mind.

"I don't got a name," he says, still not looking at me.

"So what shall I call you?"

He's walking away already but he stops, turns, and looks down at me. He shrugs. "Whatever you like," he says.

"Whatever You Like? Can we make it Whatever for short?"

Something is bulging, almost bursting inside me, and for a second I feel as if I might cry, as if this boy turning away and leaving me alone again is going to trigger some kind of mental collapse, but he smiles and the pressure in my chest begins to recede. Not a whole smile, not even really half a smile, but something. It isn't a scowl, anyway. For a flicker of an instant, his gaze meets mine; his restless, sad gray eyes look into mine. I've made contact, human to human. And it strikes me that though I e-mail America every day, though I often phone France, read tweets from Canada and Australia and India, though I watch films and connect with websites from everywhere on the planet, I have never before really looked into the eyes of a kid like this.

Children on Ritalin are said to become less fidgety in class and to show an improvement in 'behaviour which is perceived by teachers as disruptive and socially inappropriate'. No wonder that ADHD soon began to be diagnosed on the basis of school-teachers' reports and was observed to show a peculiar expression pattern, often remitting at weekends and in school holidays...The clear implication is that, whatever it does for the child, Ritalin makes life more comfortable for harassed teachers and parents.

Steven Rose, *The 21st Century Brain*

TROY

Can we make it Whatever for short? he says.

I never spoke to someone like him before—someone posh—except for maybe social workers, but they ain't proper posh like this guy. It's kind of weird that even now tied up he's trying to be funny, but it's obvious why. He wants me on his side. Chat me up, talk me around—silver tongue—thick kid—twist me around his finger—that's what he's thinking. I should smack him one for trying it on, but he's just a guy tied up—I can see he's shitting bricks—and I can see the effort he's making to mask the fear. Been there myself enough times—different situation, same principle—working every muscle to act normal to stop someone wanting to hurt you. That's what makes me feel sorry for him, almost. Don't know why, it just does.

Till now I've given him nothing, just been proper cold—not 'cause I think he could slick me, just 'cause that's what you got to do. I seen it on TV—all hostage stuff ends the same—they get you talking and once you relax you're vulnerable—that's how it goes every time. The hero cop tied up sweating like a pig but acting calm—making friends until the moment the dumb-ass kidnapper drops his guard and leaves the gun/knife/phone within grabbing distance. Always the same story, but you've got to be thick to think the person you kidnapped is your friend. I mean, obviously they hate you—it's so obvious, why would you even talk to them—why would you be nice, 'cause if they're being nice to you, they don't mean it, and if you think they do, you are pitiful.

So I should ignore him, I know. I should keep on ignoring him, but it ain't so easy. I feel a bit sorry for the guy. Whoever he works for, he's just a bloke who was doing his job. It's not like he's personally done anything to deserve what's happening to him—at least no more than anyone else—no more than all the millions of people who have easy lives and act like people who don't are stupid or lazy or invisible or whatever. It's everyone, not just this guy we got.

Don't really know why, but I stop on the way out and turn back. I look at him trying to tell him with my eyes I don't hate him—but I can't let myself talk to him. Nothing personal, I just can't.

I won't forget what you did, he says. *It was you that saved me.*

What you talking about? I ain't even choosing to talk to him, but the words sort of speak themselves.

He was going to stab me. You stopped him.

He wasn't going to stab you.

It looked to me like he was. But you stopped him. Do you understand what that means?

'Course I understand.

I'm not sure you do.

You kidding me? I ain't staying. I ain't talking to you.

When this is over, and you kids are on trial, you're the only one that stands a chance of getting off.

Don't talk shit.

What, you think you're going to keep me here forever? You think nobody's looking for me? You think the police are just going to let you all go?

He's pushing it now— disrespecting me, taking it too far. This ain't right. I got to put him in his place and get out. Can't let him mess with my head—it's me that's got to mess with his head. *How do you know we'll let* you *go?* I say—quiet but proper threatening.

He don't even pause, don't look surprised or nothing. He ain't so much of a pussy as he looks. *I don't. Which is why we can help each other.*

No, we can't.

If I get hurt, you're done for like the rest of them. If we help each other, there's something in it for both of us.

You think I'm thick.

I think your friends might be, but I think maybe you're not. Which is why we can help each other.

I stare him down—don't want him to think he's got to me. I know it's all bullshit, but part of me's got to know what he means. For a second it's like I'm on a cloud—no body, no floor under me, nothing—just my thoughts, my eyes staring at him and him staring back. I don't want to say nothing, but I got to ask—I can't not ask. *What you talking about?*

I'm just saying, you help me and I'll help you.

My friends ain't thick. I got a weird feeling in my stomach like I'm being a traitor or something for listening to his brain-twisting bullshit. It's like I knew it would be—just

53

what I told myself can't happen, but now I've fallen for it. He's popped seeds into my head that I don't want—poison seeds I can't get out once they're in—can't stop them growing, neither. He's devious, man, a proper snake.

You're a good person, he says. *I can see it. I can see that you're different.*

I roll up a ball of saliva and spit it *splat* near his feet. *Different from what?*

Are you saying you're not?

Not what?

Different.

Everyone's different. You think them others is all the same? They're not. You don't mean different. You mean better. You're trying to make me think I'm better than them just like you think you're better than me. Well, you ain't, and I ain't.

He smiles, but not a proper smile—more a scared smile.

Why you smiling?

You're smart.

Is that all you think about? Who's better than who? No wonder you work where you work.

The guy with the cornrows? Is he in charge?

What do you mean in charge?

You know what I mean.

No one's in charge.

There's no leader?

What is there to lead?

You're not a gang?

No.

So what are you?

We're pissed off.

About what? About Concentr8?

About everything.

It was that guy's idea to kidnap me, wasn't it? It was him that got you into all this.

All what?

You know what I mean.

He's twice the man you'll ever be, you dick. Everyone respects him. Everyone. Who respects you? Can you think of anyone? Can you think of one person?

He shrugs and I don't even know what the shrug means. Maybe he just feels the conversation turning bad. He looks away and suddenly acts as if he's alone. He ain't going to answer the question, and it wasn't even a question anyway.

I turn and walk off, not quite sure what I've done—'cause I know that conversation was like a contest, and I don't know who won and who lost. He's trying to play me and maybe he managed it, maybe he didn't. I got to be careful, he's slippery; not like the dickweed he looks.

LEE

chairs, man, I mean sitting on the floor, that's for animals, ain't it

so I got a load from upstairs, that weird room with just a table in it, but not nice ones and one with wheels on it that's a laugh 'cause you can shove yourself around on it and other people too

but I keep looking, man, don't give up even though the others've stopped

through the back there's this closed off outside bit, small and dark loads of cigarette ends and a garbage pile and it's right there on top

an armchair

purple, big, super-comfy like a throne or something

climb up over all the junk just one thought in my head—
get that chair

shove it down, falls with a smack

turn it right way up and it smells a bit 'cause it's been outside for I don't know, ages or something, but in this weather it's dry, everything is

few springs poking through, but so what

sit on it

bit pricky on the ass but feels good to sit proper

like in a lounge, like we got our own place just for us

drag it in

only one wheel underneath, other three all busted just
metal spikes that scrape on the ground carving scratches

makes it move in a weird spiral whichever way you push it

kills my back, I swear, but I know the others are going to
be real pleased I found it, like proper impressed

but I'm just going in when there's this moment and everyone jumps up but not toward me, in another direction

so I go and look and it's Matchstick

Blaze's little brother

just turned up

it's 'cause he's like a little version of Blaze, that's why he's
Matchstick, and also 'cause he's so skinny

like he almost ain't there, that's how skinny

but now he's here and he got pizzas 'cause it turns out
Blaze texted him or something and they been here together
a while back just checking the place out so he knew where
we was

but he ain't told no one

and when Blaze said come, he did

lifted money, got food, don't know if he's staying or what

and when there's a gap in all the talking I say, *I found a chair*

and they all turn and look at it but just for a second

and Blaze says, *bit shit, ain't it*

then we eat the pizza

and later I push the chair into the circle and it ain't shit, I
know it ain't

but nobody says nothing

After I've had Ritalin every time I'm like omg where's my
phone what's on twitter what's on instagram omg text text
tweet tweet omg can't stop

Twitter

KAREN

If you said to me at the beginning, *This is what we're going to
do, are you up for it?* I would have said, *No way, man, are you
crazy?* But then when things just roll out, with Blaze all
focused, I don't know, the whole thing carries you along,
and at each moment it makes sense, then suddenly you find
yourself somewhere and you're just thinking, *WHAT THE
FUCK?* You know?

Maybe the others are regretting it, I don't know. I mean,
I'm not actually *regretting* it, but it is a bit weird? I mean, I
trust Blaze and everything, but in a way he's screwed us.
'Cause we're all in this, but none of us was asked or consulted
or nothing.

Troy thinks Blaze is God, he's so up his ass I know he
ain't doubting nothing, and Lee is, like, I mean, he's just
vacant, so that don't even count, but sometimes I look at
Femi and I think maybe he wants out, maybe he ain't really
into what's happened.

Troy was in there for ages. Earlier? Giving the guy his
food? I mean, how long is that supposed to take? I swear
he's slippery. Came out all shifty-eyed, not looking at nobody.
I'm watching him every step; he ain't going to get away with
nothing.

It's the way he looks at me when I'm with Blaze that does my head in. I mean, guys look at me, all guys, that's just the way it is. I'm used to it, don't mind, it's kind of a power, ain't it? Over guys? I mean, half of them'll do whatever you want if you just put on the right voice and act like you're into them, even if you ain't? Pathetic, but it works.

But Troy's different? His eyes are cold, sucking in other people and judging them but giving nothing back, and it's like he's looking right into me, where he's seen something rotten or—I don't know, it just creeps me out he's such a freak.

I swear, there's something wrong with him, some kind of silent thing between him and Blaze and it goes both ways. I don't know what they got on each other, but whatever happens between me and Blaze—and *everything* has happened, believe me, everything, every which way, with a cherry on top—I sometimes feel it ain't me that's in his heart. It's not like I need Blaze to love me, or expect it, 'cause what does that even mean anyway, but it's just kind of weird the way him and Troy look at each other and talk to each other and know what the other's thinking. I ain't jealous or nothing, but sometimes I get the vibe that Blaze almost loves him? Not in a batty way, I ain't saying that, I'm just saying it ain't normal and Troy's such a little prick it don't make no sense.

They go way back almost like brothers, so can't nobody get between them, but that don't mean Troy can act like I ain't good enough. I swear, him thinking that, it makes me want to stab him. Not literally, just in my head, like a YouTube video to cheer yourself up or something. Instead of kittens and shit.

So when nobody's looking I go in and look at the hostage? To see? I swear, he looks about five years older than the day before, and it's the sight of him that makes me realize we've gone too far. This can't do us no good. There ain't no way out of what we done, and there ain't no way out of getting caught, neither. Sooner or later, we going to pay.

I ain't like the others; I mean, I'm a trainee, I got something to lose. Blaze and Troy, it don't mean nothing to them to give up—fall off the edge—'cause no offense, but that's already happened, ain't it? Me, I got plans, so it don't make no sense to be part of this. I mean, it's the worst job in the world, just sweeping up hair all day, literally the most boring thing you can think of, but sometimes I get to assist on a weave or something, and once a week I do some practice cuts, so when I'm starting to think I can't take it no more, I remind myself there's a point eventually. It's my aunt got me in, so I have to act all grateful, even when the highlight of my week is standing there for an hour holding dead bits of cut-off hair, and she talks down to me so badly half the time I'm on the edge of telling her to just fuck off and walking out, but still, I'm trying not to. Point is, I got a career. Not like the others. If I get arrested, that's the end of everything.

I ain't even touched the hostage, not once—ain't done nothing except been in the wrong place when stuff was happening.

He looks so rough—scared shitless when I walk in—and he watches me but don't speak. Not the look I'd normally get from a guy like this—the looking-but-pretending-not-to-look eyes like you get on the bus all the time. Or the others that just stare shameless at every part of you, and don't even care, and you got to look away yourself. Half of them old enough to be my dad, but that don't even stop them. Can't see none of that the way he stares up at me from the radiator, tied up like a dog. Maybe that's what it takes to stop a guy thinking with his dick.

Hard to explain, but for a moment I feel almost like I'm afraid of how weak he is. It's like having some tiny pet that'll die if you don't feed him. It's power, but a scary power that leaves you feeling weak about how strong you are. You know? Maybe that's bullshit, but…

I'd sort of forgot it, but now when I look down at him I remember what I said the day before when we was taking him. That one moment? Didn't even mean it or nothing, but it came out of my mouth, didn't it? *Get him! Just get him!* Don't even know what I was thinking or why I said it, but I can hear the words again now, echoing in my head, as if it's someone else saying them, but it ain't, it's me.

If I could take it back—delete it—I would, 'cause I know you can get done for stuff like that. Just saying things—mouthing off for a laugh—the feds can turn that into a crime if they want to, if they got it in for you, which they have.

You all right? I say. Don't know why. Can't think of nothing else.

He just nods. Stupid, really, since he obviously ain't.

Got water?

He nods.

It's going to be okay, I say, and I still don't even know what I mean or why I'm saying it, but maybe I'm just trying to show him I ain't a bad person. 'Cause this is going to be over at some point and I don't want him to think I'm a killer or a psycho or something. It wasn't me who started this, I just got sucked into it, and he has to know that.

He don't move, smile, blink, nothing.

He works people, Blaze, makes them scared of him. That's his thing. But he don't do nothing, hardly ever.

That's his name? he says. *Blaze?*

My heart starts beating fast now, 'cause I know I messed up.

NO! I say. *'Course it ain't. What you talking about?*

Sorry. I thought—

Fuck you!

Almost kick him, don't know why, the anger just flares up, rockets into me, so instead I walk out, banging the door after me.

What you doing in there? says Femi. He's right there outside the door, like he was listening. Nearly walk right into him.

Nothing. What's it to you?

Is he okay?

See for yourself.

Then there's like a long weird moment when Femi's looking at me and I'm looking at him and it's almost as if he's asking me to bail, asking me to just run for it with him, maybe even go to the feds, just do whatever we got to do to get out of this without being locked up for the rest of our lives. And I'm almost with him? I'm that close. I almost say it. But before anything comes out of my mouth there's the megaphone. It's like a joke? Not 'cause it's funny. Just—I mean—do these guys get their lines from TV, or what?

This is the police, it says. *You are surrounded.*

Femi starts running around, shouting, *What the fuck? What are we going to do? I told you this was going to happen!*

I start freaking even worse. I'm just going, *How'd they find us? How'd they find us?*

Lee goes up to the window of the office and starts shouting over and over: *THEY'RE OUTSIDE! THE FEDS! THEY'RE OUTSIDE! THEY'RE OUTSIDE!*

Matchstick's quiet and still, but his face has gone all big and puffy like he's fighting himself not to cry.

Only two people stay calm. Blaze and Troy. Blaze looks at Troy, Troy looks back at Blaze, and in the corner of Troy's mouth there's a little curl. Not a smile, but something that looks like it's thinking about turning into one?

It's like they planned for this and they know what to do next and I swear, it vexes me so bad the way them two always know what each other is thinking when I never have a clue? Not that I'd want to know what's going on in Troy's pissy little brain, but if Blaze just let me in and told me the shit he tells Troy, I swear to God the two of us would be so powerful, together we'd be able to do anything, and nothing would never come between us. But that ain't going to happen. It just ain't. If you ask me, I reckon that's the only thing Blaze is afraid of.

Back in the 1930s, Aldous Huxley's prescient *Brave New World* offered a universal panacea, a drug called Soma that removed all existential pain. Today's Brave New World will have a multitude of designer psychotropics, available either by consumer choice (so called 'smart' drugs to enhance cognition) or by state prescription (Ritalin for behaviour control).

Steven Rose, *The 21st Century Brain*

THE NEGOTIATOR

"This is the police," I say. "You are surrounded."

It is important to be clear. Surrounded, perhaps, is an exaggeration. The entrance to the facility is fully policed, as is most of the perimeter, but the rear frontage onto the railway tracks is presenting logistical difficulties as yet unsurmounted. Truthfulness can sometimes be sacrificed in the interests of clarity, though the buildup of trust between negotiator and hostage-taker cannot be underestimated as a crucial element in attaining satisfactory resolutions.

As is usual in these situations, no immediate response is forthcoming.

All eyes are on me. An armed unit is at the scene, guns at the ready, but I bide my time. For several minutes, I do nothing and say nothing. Successful police work is as much about what you don't do as what you do do. One could say the same about pleasuring a woman, but I shan't get into that here.

"We know exactly where you are," I say (also not entirely true), "and we just want to talk to you." (Definitely not true. We want to lock up the little bastards and throw away the key.)

Another long silence.

"I am a negotiator from the Metropolitan Police."

A head appears at a high window. "Fuck off," she says.

First contact usually follows a similar path, though I must say this girl is unusually succinct.

"We want to help you," I say.

"Like fuck you do."

"Do you have access to food and water?"

Not what you would have said in the circumstances, no doubt, but you haven't had the benefit of my training and experience.

"What?"

"Have you got any food and water? I need to know you are okay," I continue, megaphone to lips, "and I need to know your hostage is okay. That is my first priority. After that, we can talk." Note the simplistic but non-patronizing vocabulary. Textbook.

She disappears from the window. There is a long silence, then a new face appears. A boy in a green T-shirt. White, skinny, unwashed hair, acne at the corners of his mouth. The following is not a term whose usage I condone, but this kid is pure trash. Which is hardly a surprise. I mean, who else would do anything this brainless?

"Nando's," he barks.

"What?"

"Nando's. Jumbo Platter. Two of them. And some chicken burgers and fries and steak. And Concentr8. Shitloads of it. Fifty packets."

"I'm not sure we can do that."

"You've got an hour. After that we'll…we'll…cut one of his toes off."

I can dimly hear laughter emanate from the window. A different face appears. "And Coke and Red Bull and Lucozade Sport. Loads of it. Or we'll do a finger."

More laughter. I decide this is a prudent moment to terminate our dialogue and phone the head office.

A few hours later, I give my first press conference. I'm quite used to such events, to the frenzy of excitement, to the illusion a few cameras and TV lights produce that the whole world is watching you. The most important thing is to avoid, at all costs, giving the impression that you might be enjoying yourself. Though, of course, I am.

Appalling crimes are taking place all over the city, but today this is the top story. There's nothing quite like a hostage crisis to get news editors going. It's never a hostage situation, never a hostage event. Always a hostage crisis.

The room is crammed with journalists—every chair taken, every inch of carpet space fought over—and the air is stifling. All the windows are open, but they may as well not be, because nothing is moving. From floor to ceiling, it's just 100 percent exhaled journo-breath. Not pleasant. (This isn't a question of halitosis—merely of oxygen supply. The aroma is the usual conference-room stew of deodorant, perfume, and coffee. Journalists, I hate to admit, probably have the edge over my own profession on the personal hygiene front.)

I deliver a short statement.

"Ladies and gentlemen, good evening. Significant progress was made today in the case of Anthony Paxton. His abduction from in front of the mayor's office has been confirmed. His abductors have been cornered and are in the process of being identified and traced. An area around the abandoned warehouses formerly used by Bundren Panel Beaters in Hackney has been cordoned off, inside of which a negotiation is under way. The full range of police assets has been put into this equation, including armed officers, and I would like to remind members of the press to respect this cordon at all costs. Direct verbal contact with the hostage has not yet been established, but we are confident of his whereabouts and that he is in good health. The hostage-takers are young, and are believed to be part of the citywide unrest that has flared up in the last week. Their demands, as yet, are obscure, but we are confident Mr. Paxton can be extracted soon. However, we need to take a measured approach to achieve this without incurring unnecessary risk to his person. These situations are known to evolve according to unpredictable and fast-changing patterns, and we are therefore proceeding with extreme caution."

Questions fly in, flashbulbs pop, microphones and Dictaphones are shoved in my face. Were I of a vain temperament, which is the precise antithesis of my nature, it might occur to me that the sensation is somewhat akin to being, for a brief while, some kind of movie star. But of course such thoughts could not be farther from my mind. I am a police officer, a seasoned professional who is always focused on the humble task of protecting the public and bringing criminals to justice. These people may be clamoring after every syllable that drops from my lips, but I never allow myself to forget that I am their servant.

I shan't dwell on the exact questions: they are always the same, always shrill, always ignorant of the patience required in following the procedural demands of effective police work. In highly dramatic circumstances, with a tinderbox of malcontented youth ready to be provoked into costly conflagrations by a single inopportune comment from a uniformed officer, a conference of this type must be tackled with near surgical precision.

I nearly slip up once, almost allowing the words "lazy, ungrateful scum" to slip out, but I rein myself in and manage to summon up a more PC formulation. Other than that, I think I put in a damn good performance.

Cognitive enhancers and Ritalin exemplify two important features of the psychocivilised society into which we are moving: on the one hand its essential individualism, on the other, increasingly sophisticated methods of control and seemingly non-violent coercion.

Steven Rose, *The 21st Century Brain*

THE JOURNALIST

"Officer Densworth! Officer Densworth!" It's always good to use their name. You're far more likely to be picked. "Officer Densworth!"

"Yes? Over there." He points at me. Being female doesn't do any harm, either.

"Thank you. I'm interested to know if you've singled out a cause for the rioting."

"Well, these people, they're a bunch of ... I mean ... there are ... I mean, social issues can be a factor, of course ... but that's a matter for the politicians. My job, and the job of my colleagues throughout the force ... I mean the service ... the police service ... is to uphold law and order, which under very testing circumstances we are striving to achieve insomuch as our capacities at the present time will allow."

I dive in with the follow-up before the last word is out of his mouth. "Do you support the change of government policy on Concentr8? Since this was clearly the trigger for the rioting, do you think its reintroduction would be the quickest way to return calm to the streets?"

"Again, that's a matter for the politicians."

"Do you hold the mayor responsible?"

"I … er … I'm here to answer questions on police matters. Next, please. You, sir."

Predictable. Sometimes the point isn't to get an answer. Just asking the question is a way of putting an idea into play. *When asked if he held the mayor responsible, Officer Densworth declined to comment.* Job done. You've blamed the mayor.

The press conference rattles on, the policeman in front of the mikes lapping up his fifteen minutes of fame, relishing each opportunity to pick one journalist from the howling, begging pack, but nobody has an intelligent question, and he doesn't offer any interesting answers.

I'm first out of the door, and I know exactly where I'm going.

The offices of Professor Pyle aren't what I expected. The address in west London, on one of the busy roads out toward the airport, is hardly impressive, but the building turns out to be a glass-fronted low-rise office block, discreetly costly, recently built in the international corporate a-little-bit-modern-but-nothing-risky style. The building is set back from the road, behind a small parking lot jammed with high-end luxury sedans and a wisp of pseudo-Japanese garden. If I'd had to guess what this place housed, I probably would have gone for a secretive hedge fund. It's the opposite, in other words, of a university campus.

Pyle's secretary greets me with a smile that is without approval, disapproval, curiosity, recognition, or warmth. She has exceptionally good teeth, the kind that could make short work of rare steak, though they probably haven't bitten into anything more nourishing than a salad for weeks.

"Do you have an appointment?" she says through pursed lips. These people can sniff out a journalist and they don't like us. An expression somewhere between surprise and mild dismay settles on her features when I give her a name that corresponds to the next meeting on her calendar.

As she ushers me into the adjoining office, I thank her with as much insincerity as I can load onto two words.

Pyle is a small man behind a large desk. He wears rimless glasses and has a line of closely cropped hair at the outer limits of his head, like the stripe of seaweed you find along a beach at low tide. He has no lips, just a horizontal, expressionless slot under his nose—an orifice that looks less suited to eating or kissing than to the insertion of a CD-ROM.

His office is not so much air-conditioned as refrigerated. He stands and extends an arm across his desk. "Ms. . . . ?"

"Giotta."

It's a curious handshake—my hand hot and sweaty; his cold and dry.

"Giotta? Are you Italian?" he asks, his voice all pub quiz smug.

"No. British."

"But your family?" He's persistent, still staking a claim for that pub quiz point.

"My grandfather. One of them."

"Your father's father."

The man is a genius. There's something about this interchange that gives me a sense of how I should play the interview. Fragile ego. Wants to be right. Wants to be Daddy. There's a playbook for this kind of person, and I have a sense it isn't going to be hard. I warm up my smile and ask if I can take a seat.

"Sicily," I say, shifting my voice a little higher than usual. "Have you ever been there?"

"No, but I often take my wife to…" And he's off. Everyone has something to say about Italy. I do lots of oh-reallying, that-sounds-deliciousing, and how-fascinatinging. After ten minutes of this, his posture and tone of voice have changed completely. He thinks we're friends. He's forgotten that the mayor's office forced him into taking the meeting. He's forgotten I'm there to catch him out. In dog-speak, I've got him on his back and I'm tickling his tummy, all before I've uttered my first question. It's perfect. If you can get your interviewee to mistake your interview for a cozy chat between friends, you're going to hit pay dirt. It's not often, these days, you can find someone dumb enough to fall for it. Sometimes I forget this technique is even possible.

"Do you mind if I record? I'm really sorry, it's protocol these days."

"No problem. Go ahead."

I put the Dictaphone carefully out of his eye line.

"I'm doing a piece on the mayor and there were a few technicalities on the subject of Concentr8 that he wasn't in a position to answer, so he put me onto you. He described you as the leading authority."

"Well, that's very nice of him, but I…well…I suppose he's probably right. It is my area, and he hired me to be the Youth Mental Health Tsar, if you like. I mean, that wasn't the official job title, but that's how I came to be seen."

I smile and lean toward him, sensing that I don't even need to ask any questions. The best tactic is to just let him off the leash and see where he leads me.

"You see, for decades, centuries, we've treated youth crime simply as a matter for the police. Experts like myself, who have dedicated our lives to the treatment of troubled youngsters, were simply ignored. There is a wealth of methods available to the modern clinician for helping young people who are distracted, hyperactive, or unproductive back onto the straight and narrow. The connection between young people exhibiting these behaviors and people who fall down in the employment market is incontrovertible. And from there, you're into petty crime, gang culture, etc."

"Stick rather than carrot?"

"Exactly. The traditional approach is all stick and no carrot. Hugo Nelson was the first politician to act on the idea that you have to help these people *before* they begin to help themselves in socially destructive ways." He pokes the table on the word *before*, in a gesture that looks like his version of passionate animation. "The symptoms of criminality can be treated before they develop into the full-blown disease."

"So you're a pioneer in making a connection between mental health and crime?"

"I wouldn't say pioneer. But I am one of the few people in this area who's been lucky enough to have the ear of a policy maker with real budgets at his disposal, and a desire to take action."

"So you were pleased to have a chance to help young people who you thought were likely to end up on the wrong side of the law?"

He smiles, revealing for the first time the presence of human lips. "Exactly. ADHD is reaching epidemic proportions throughout the Western world, and children who aren't helped with this issue are at enormous risk of failing at school and subsequently failing at life. Disruptive children, put on Ritalin, can be pacified within days, sometimes hours. The downward trajectory of their lives can be halted, just like that. The trouble is, Ritalin requires three doses a day. This new drug, Concentr8, is a huge leap forward. It lasts eight hours rather than four, hence the name, which eliminates the need for a child to self-medicate during school, along with all the uncertainties that introduces. Other long-acting drugs have been around for a while, but they've always been expensive. Concentr8 is cheap. It's the wonder drug the entire field has been waiting for. That's why I recommended its use to the mayor, and was delighted when he took up my proposal so wholeheartedly."

"So was the idea yours or his?"

He spreads his arms, palms upward, pompous-humble. "Well, of course, the mayor is the policy maker. After the last riots he commissioned me to do a wide-ranging study and come up with a proposal for a forward course of action. I'm simply an advisor, trying to do his job."

"What were the parameters of the study?"

"Well, it was a question of what we could do to get these wild kids under control. Blue-sky thinking. My conclusion was that with a cheaper drug than Ritalin now on the market, we didn't in fact need to do anything new. We just needed to find the political will, and the budget, to extend what we were already doing."

"Extend what, exactly?"

"Well, difficult children...I mean...sufferers from ADHD...have been prescribed Ritalin for considerable time. This has proved highly effective, and the numbers of children receiving this help has been going up year after year. It's been the case for a long time that if your child gets an ADHD diagnosis, the parent becomes eligible for disability living allowance. All I did was point out to the mayor that the existing policy was the perfect incentive scheme for containing the kind of children who go on to exhibit anti-social behaviors. With this cheaper drug, and a more proactive approach, I felt like we could make inroads into new areas, and produce tangible results for society as a whole."

He's perched on the front of his seat again, back in table-poking mode. I notice for the first time that his desk is entirely clear. Not one pen, no lamp, no paper, not even a phone. Just one laptop moored on a lake of glistening cherry-brown wood.

"And how did you do that?"

"The key element was the idea of sending mental health visitors to schools rather than insisting that children travel to a separate location to get an assessment. This had a huge effect on destigmatizing the diagnosis. That, and greater clarity in explaining the benefits system to parents."

"So is this a question of mental health or social control?"

"Both. It's about joining the dots."

"Between medicine and policing?"

He coughs, as if a fragment of gourmet food has unexpectedly gone down the wrong way, detecting for the first time a note of potential criticism in my voice.

"No. Absolutely not. Those two areas are quite separate. But if you step back from the situation and think about these issues in an intelligent way, you begin to see that where you have mental-health-related destructive behaviors spreading widely through certain communities, the question is as much of sick individuals as a sick society. And only if doctors join hands with politicians do we stand a chance of really solving the problem."

"Thank you so much," I say. "That was great. So kind of you to give up your time."

"My pleasure. If you have any other questions..."

I pick up the Dictaphone, click it off, and place it in my bag. "Oh no. You've been great. And if you remember the name of that pizza place in Venice, do let me know. My e-mail's on there." I hand him a card. "It's such a beautiful city, isn't it?"

"Oh, exquisite. Quite wonderful."

I leave slowly. More on Venice. Lots of attentive listening to his theories on the psychological effects of water, on Renaissance art, on Italian coffee... blah blah blah.

At the door, as if it's an afterthought, I turn back. "Oh, one last thing. I was just wondering. You said psychiatrists were sent to schools. Did they assess all the kids, or just some?"

"Oh, you couldn't assess everyone. That would take forever. I think the head teachers put forward a list and made the appointments. I mean, they know who the bad kids are, don't they?"

"The bad kids?"

"Troubled. I mean, the teachers spot the symptoms, the heads collate the information; it's the only logical way of doing it."

"And what proportion of the selected kids were diagnosed?"

"Oh, you'll have to ask the mayor that, but the uptake was excellent. The preselection process was very effective. It's an excellent scheme, and I can't say I'm surprised that its withdrawal has created this uproar."

"So you see a direct connection between the withdrawal of Concentr8 and the riots?"

"Absolutely. Doesn't everyone? I'm not condoning their behavior, but we have the means to keep these people quiet and just to let that all go is ludicrous."

"Are there withdrawal symptoms related to coming off Concentr8?"

"It's hard to be categorical about these things, but just a return to the symptoms exhibited before being given the drug, spread over a large number of unruly young people at the same time, was likely to create a highly combustible situation. The prime minister has a lot to answer for. Off the record, of course."

Off the record? What a schmuck. It's the old put-away-the-Dictaphone-then-carry-on-the-conversation trick. Works every time.

"Thanks again," I say. "I won't waste any more of your day."

"Not at all."

It could be my imagination, but as I shake his hand I momentarily sense a flicker of panic scampering across his features.

It is much cheaper to tranquilize distraught housewives living in isolation in tower-blocks with nowhere for their children to play than to demolish these blocks and to rebuild on a human scale, or even to provide play-groups. The drug industry, the government, the pharmacist, the tax-payer, and the doctor all have vested interests in "medicalizing" socially determined stress responses.

M. Lader, 'Benzodiazepines—the opium of the masses?' *Neuroscience*

TROY

The food and medication you requested has been placed outside. In return we would like some evidence of the good health of the hostage. A walkie-talkie is there to facilitate this.

It's the megaphone.

Nando's! yells Lee, jumping up and rushing straight out to get the stuff. Before anyone has time to say it might be a trick or cover your face or any of the obvious shit like that, he's gone. For a moment I'm thinking that's the last we're going to see of him—then he's back and there's enough food for ten, I swear—plus drinks and a ton of Concentr8. Everything we asked for. Unbelievable.

What we gonna do with this? he says, holding out the walkie-talkie.

Everyone looks at Blaze, but he just shrugs.

We going to need more meals, I say. *Let's do it. Keep them sweet.*

Suit yourself, he says with a flick of his chin that's telling Lee to pass it to me.

Lee's happy to hand it over—like it's toxic or something.

I walk off with the walkie-talkie but turn back near the door and shout, *Don't eat it all without me* even though that ain't even possible. Sometimes just walking away from the others feels spooky—especially when it's to go in to the hostage.

Never used a walkie-talkie before. Didn't know they even still existed. Seen them on TV, though. People saying *over* at the end of each sentence for no reason. I ain't doing that—that's stupid.

The guy looks up at me from the radiator. So depressing, man, the sight of him. Ain't his fault, though. I ain't never been to a zoo, but I don't reckon I'd even want to. Same thing. Animals all caged up—how are you supposed to enjoy that?

They want to talk to you, I say.

I know. I heard.

Just say you're okay. Say we ain't hurt you. Nothing else.

All right.

Anything else and we'll…you know…just don't say nothing more.

I won't.

I click the chunky button at the side and it hisses like a TV.

You there?

We're here. Please may we speak to the hostage? Over.

Over? What a dick! I put it to the guy's mouth.

This is Anthony. I'm okay. They haven't hurt me.

I pull it away before he can say anything else. *Bye,* I say, walking out and heading for the Nando's. Don't want to miss the good stuff.

I'm about to sit down and eat when Blaze says, *Smash it.*

What?

Might be bugged. Don't need it no more.

I'll chuck it out the back.

I go to the back door fast, 'cause I swear it physically hurts walking away from all that food. Shove open the big folding door onto a little closed-in smoking area and chuck out the walkie-talkie but sliding it, not tossing it, 'cause I don't want it to smash. Don't know why—just you never know. Best to have it there in case. Especially if I'm the only one who knows where it is. Wouldn't want Femi to get it.

It's thinking about Femi that makes me step out and shove it under some bricks. Hidden is definitely better.

Everyone's already had a Concentr8 and you wouldn't believe the amount of food that's already gone by the time I get back, but there's still enough. It's more comfy now than the night before, 'cause we been all over the warehouse gathering stuff up to make a base. There's a load of chairs from some room up near the office—almost like school ones but better, 'cause they're a bit cushioned. One of them's on wheels and we been messing around with it half the afternoon, playing like human tennis or something, putting somebody onto it and shoving them between two people fast as you can—or just crashing them into things to see what happens. It was a good laugh except when Lee got gashed across the forehead on a shelf—but he didn't mind that much and didn't even want to stop. Sometimes with Lee it's almost like he wants to get hurt. For the extra attention or something. Just makes everyone think he's more of an idiot, but he don't get that.

There's also an armchair that got found somewhere and dragged in. It's messed up with springs poking out and it twangs when you sit down, but it's still better than the others, so that's where Blaze sits. Nobody says nothing, we just know that's Blaze's chair.

Should have aksed for some White Ace, says Lee.

No chance you dick, says Karen.

Why not?

'Cause it's the feds! They'd have to arrest themselves for giving it to us!

Everyone laughs, even Blaze.

Femi ain't with us. He's on his own up in the room we got the chairs from. Nothing in there now except some massive desk big as a parking space. He's been weird all day. Went up there more than an hour ago—either sleeping or sulking, nobody knows—and he ain't even come down for the food.

I get up—rearrange the buckets to put two thighs and a couple of fistfuls of fries into one—and I take it up to him with a Lucozade.

He's on that table lying down like it's a bed. Don't know if he was asleep or awake, but he sits up when he hears the door.

I give him the food but don't say nothing. I ain't acting angry, but not too friendly, neither. Don't want nobody to think I'm taking sides or nothing, least of all against Blaze. I just put it down next to him and walk out fast so nobody can say I stopped to talk to him. Don't blame him for feeling weird or for saying what he said. But I can't have nobody thinking I want to go over to his side, 'cause that ain't me—that just ain't even possible.

It was all a bit flat, a bit weird before the food, but after we've eaten and had a pill, everyone's up and buzzing. Lee's been eating his food walking around 'cause he hates sitting down, and suddenly there's this huge crash and you can hear his stupid laugh.

Watch this, he says, and he picks up a huge metal thing almost as big as his arm—some massive wrench or something—and chucks it against the tire rack hard as he can. Makes this massive noise and the metal shelf takes a huge dent.

Looks like a good laugh, so I walk over and have a turn—then Matchstick does even though he can't hardly lift it—then Blaze, too. It ends up with Matchstick and Blaze on one side and me and Lee on the other—and we're chucking this huge thing at each other and I swear, if it hit you, it would kill you—it's such a laugh. Whatever it hits, there's like a boom unless it's the concrete, and even then half the time it takes a chip out of it before it skids away. Karen watches but don't join in—and I don't see him coming, but after a bit Femi's there too and he goes on Blaze's side, which I reckon is a good thing. Except that now me and Lee's outnumbered, so I go behind one of the big machines and Lee makes a pile of old tires 'cause we're in that corner. One of the tires he takes must have been holding up the stack, 'cause there's this sudden topple and masses of tires come down—almost bury him—and some just roll out all over the place, it's crazy—and this wrench is just flying back and forward smashing things up—the noise of it almost like a war zone. I swear, if the feds is listening they're just going to be going, *What the fuck?*

Blaze and Matchstick and Femi's behind a huge shelf thing now, but there's a gap at the top, so me and Lee are tossing it high—high as we can so it comes looping down on top of them. I swear, it takes a chunk out of the concrete where it lands and it's good nobody gets hit, 'cause I don't know what we'd do.

After that, tires start getting chucked about everywhere, then Femi figures out a hubcap works like a Frisbee if you throw it right, and there's just stuff flying everywhere—all of us laughing—Blaze close to Matchstick, always making sure he don't get hit.

Everyone's forgot about Karen but then there's this fluttery noise and we all look up, and she's on the balcony outside the office and she's got armfuls of papers from somewhere, and there ain't really no reason for it, but she's chucking them down. It's like some snowstorm or something, it's just beautiful. Papers everywhere, flipping, flapping—some of them going miles. It makes us stop chucking stuff and we all end up underneath her and she goes in and out of the office—chucks down more and more paper—and we just stand under there like it's rain and we're cooling off in it or something. Might sound stupid, but it makes me think this is the first time since we came here that we all felt proper together, like no splits or worries or arguments or nothing—just all of us a unit, feeling the same thing.

By the time she's emptied out the office, the whole place looks different—tires everywhere and paper in a huge circle spreading out from where we're standing—almost like another riot's happened, but it feels good. First time we all realized this is our place now and we can do whatever we want—ain't nobody going to stop us. Ain't never had that before and don't reckon the others has, either. It's beautiful.

Blaze goes up into the office with Karen after that and Lee goes off on his own for a dump, but between you and me, I don't reckon it's a dump.

Me and Femi, we just lie down and chill. Finish the fries. It's good he came down. If it weren't for me he'd still be up there. Matchstick disappears, but that's Matchstick, ain't it. He always comes back.

Frailty 2,900

Dementia 14,100

Hyperkinetic Syndrome [ADHD] 39,500

Department for Work and Pensions. *Disability Living Allowance recipients by main disabling condition*, May 2010

THE HOSTAGE

It's the second night that gets me worried. I mean, they took me in the evening, and night seemed to fall pretty fast. It was scary—terrifying, even—but on some level it still felt like it might be some kind of prank rather than a genuine kidnapping. I had the feeling that at any moment they might get bored, or be struck by the reality of what they were doing, and set me free. But after a whole day, just sitting there tied up in the same spot from sunrise to sunset, when it begins to get dark I feel panic grip me for the first time. I haven't let myself think that I might not get out alive, haven't allowed that thought in, but now, with darkness falling, and nightmarish howls, crashes, and shouts emanating from the warehouse, it becomes impossible to keep the idea at bay.

Kids like this don't have much restraint at the best of times, but now it sounds like they've cut themselves loose from everything, drifted outward to some zone where there's no fear of anything. Through the half-open doorway I can hear their wildness rise to a higher and higher pitch, hear the manic glee as they find more things to destroy, or new ways to smash up what's already broken. And I can't help feeling that when there's nothing left out there to break, they'll turn their attention to me.

The leader, Blaze, I can see in his eyes that he's someone who knows how to inflict pain: has mastered the skills, speaks the language like a mother tongue. There's some carnivorous power in him that I sense could rise up on a whim, and crush me.

A stripe of light stretches from the door to just near my radiator, and the high window lets in a sickly glow, so it's not exactly light and not quite dark. Through the broken pane I can see what looks like a single mosaic tile of London's gray-orange night sky.

I've never felt mentally fragile in my life, never felt there was anyone piloting my brain other than me, but now I have the feeling you get on a ski slope that's a shade too hard for you. I'm in control, but only just, and something is pulling me forward, onward, downward, faster than I have the capacity to resist.

Without warning, the cacophony from the warehouse stops. I dread, and also crave, someone coming in to see me, but the silence thickens and no footsteps approach. They must have finally gone to sleep. They've gorged themselves to exhaustion on mindless destruction. That seems to be it for the day.

I sleep in tiny snatches, probably no more than five or ten minutes at a time, jerking awake again and again. My exhausted mind seems to have made the calculation that it's too much of a risk to let itself switch off.

It feels like the middle of the night, several hours after silence fell, when the door scrapes open and somebody enters. It looks from the silhouette in the doorway like it might be Blaze. I shut my eyes, pretending to be asleep. He's not the one I should talk to. Any engagement with him, even eye contact, is dangerous. He's capable of anything.

I listen to the slide and slap of his bare feet moving ever closer. When the sound of movement stops, and I begin to hear his breath, he feels so close my body flinches and my eyes snap open. Some vestigial fighting instinct has given me the impression I'm about to be punched.

He's not as close as I thought. He's two or three paces away, the sound of his breathing amplified by either the echoey space, or my terror. He's motionless, staring down at me, his face an unreadable pitiless mask, a blank with an aura of pure menace, of fearless contempt.

He gazes at me, seemingly lost in thought, not reacting to my flinch, as if my being either awake or asleep makes no difference to him whatsoever. I want to ask him what he's looking at, why he's staring, but I'm too afraid. Those questions are cues for a fight. Even though I can hardly make him out in the half-light, his body seems to crackle with the potential to inflict physical harm.

I can't just cower there, though. I have to use every opportunity to remind him and his friends that I'm a human being.

"I need the toilet," I say.

Green T-shirt kid has taken me up till now. Never Blaze.

He looks down at me for a while longer, then wordlessly bends and unties me from the radiator without releasing my wrists from the clumsy but immovable knot that joins them together. With a tilt of the head he indicates that I should walk ahead.

We shuffle through the dank, hot air of the warehouse. Since the last time I saw it, everything smashable has been smashed. The long empty shelves have been twisted and pulled free of the wall. Used tires are scattered everywhere, and one end of the warehouse seems to have been carpeted in a layer of invoices and business letters. I would never have thought this was a place capable of being vandalized, but clearly I was wrong.

Blaze doesn't let me linger, and doesn't explain what has happened. He shoves my shoulder into the gents' toilet and straight into the first cubicle, which is now so full it's almost overflowing.

We're halfway back when I turn and face him. He has a knife in his hand, a short blade, which he holds with the calm authority of someone who knows how to use it.

"Why are you doing this?" I say. "What do you want?"

He doesn't respond. Not a flicker.

"Why me? What have I done to you? How long are you going to keep me?"

He half nods, a small upward movement of the chin that seems to mean, *Shut up, turn around, and keep walking.*

"Please," I say. "Don't do this. The longer you go on, the worse it gets for you. The police are outside. Let's just end this. I'll say you didn't hurt me. I'll say it was just a prank. I mean, you haven't really done any harm. Not yet. I mean...what is this?...It's nothing, really...we can both just walk away...no harm done. Come on. I don't hate you. Please."

His eyes remain cold, hard, and distant, as if he can't even hear me.

"What's the point of this? Please. What's it going to achieve? Come on, enough's enough. Let's just get out of here. There might be a reward. If there isn't, I can try and arrange one. You've been good to me. Everyone's going a bit crazy, right now. I'll say you didn't hurt me."

"Turn around," he says.

"Please. You've got the wrong guy. I haven't done anything. I'm nothing. I'm nobody."

"Nobody's nobody."

"I just type things into a computer. I don't make any decisions. What do you want from me?"

He stares, with the expression of someone trying to summon up a distant memory, then with an open palm he slaps me across the cheek.

"Don't be such a little bitch," he says. "Man up."

I touch my hot cheek with trembling fingers. My eyes prickle with tears. He grabs my upper arm, marches me back to the radiator, and re-knots the rope, tighter than before.

Before he has even left the room, I'm sobbing.

Day Three

THE MAYOR

"Professor Pyle. Will you take the call?"

Pyle. What a momentously crap way to start the day. Being pleasant to these functionaries is one of the hardest parts of my job. Normally I'd plead a meeting, but I get a sinking feeling the moment I hear his name. It's unusual for him to call, especially first thing in the morning. I have a sixth sense for when a fresh turd is about to float into my life, and just the sound of his name gives me a whiff. Something to do with that journalist who was after him.

I snatch the phone from its cradle. "Yes?" I bark. It's good to be rude to these people. Keeps them in their place. Reminds them of the hierarchy.

"Hello, Mayor. It's me. Professor Pyle."

"I realize that. I have a secretary."

"How are you?"

"Busy."

"Yes. Of course. I was just...I have a slight..."

"Problem."

"No. Not a problem. But something has taken place that I thought, perhaps, I should run by you just to check I haven't spoken out of turn."

"Oh, what the hell have you said? I told you she just needed to check a few facts. I told you what to say."

"Yes, but she was very friendly, and…"

"She was *friendly*? Did you honestly just tell me she was *friendly*? Oh, well, that's all right, then. She can't possibly want to stitch us up and dangle us by the balls from Tower Bridge like every other journalist, then, can she? Not if she's *friendly*! What the hell did you tell her?"

"Nothing much. I was very careful, for the whole interview. It's just that we had a little chat off the record at the end, and I may have said the odd thing I shouldn't. It was bothering me in the night, and I thought I should check with you."

"*Off the record?* What do you mean, *off the record?*"

"Well, she switched off the recorder thingy, and on the way out we were chatting about this and that. You know. Vacations. I mean, it wasn't an interview at all. That was all finished."

"Stop blathering."

"Well, she asked me if I saw any connection between the withdrawal of Concentr8 and the riots, and I said I did. I mean, that's my scientific opinion. So then she asked me if I blame the prime minister, and I kind of had to say yes."

"You blamed the prime minister?"

"Yes. Sort of."

"Wonderful! Good work. It's his bloody fault and everyone should know."

"Really?"

"Of course. *I* can't say it, but the more everyone else does, the better."

"So you're not cross?"

"Of course not. You're totally wasting my bloody time and I'm supposed to be running one of the biggest cities in the world, which is currently in meltdown, but apart from that I can think of nothing I'd rather be doing than sitting here chatting with you."

"Er...okay."

"Bye, then. We must do this again soon." Sledgehammer sarcasm. My favorite kind.

"Yes, and the stuff about head teachers selecting the children for psychiatric profiling, and how almost everyone selected took up the drug, that's common knowledge, isn't it?"

"What?"

"I just mentioned it in passing. I mean, I thought everyone knew but she seemed, kind of, strangely interested in it. Which was why I had to remind her that we were off the record."

"Remind her?"

"Er...tell her."

"You told her that, then afterward asked her if it could be off the record?"

"Sort of. I mean, the recorder was off."

"YOU'RE NOT SUPPOSED TO TALK ABOUT THAT! YOU'RE A SCIENTIST! YOU TALK ABOUT THE SCIENCE. WHAT ON EARTH MADE YOU THINK YOU SHOULD OPEN YOUR TRAP ABOUT THAT?"

"We were just chatting."

"Exactly how thick *are* you? Do you understand *anything*? Do you realize how badly you have just fucked up?"

"Er…not entirely. No."

"What the hell was I doing letting you anywhere near a journalist? It's like giving a seal pup to a shark."

"That's actually very insulting. I am a highly respected —"

"If this blows up on us, I'm going to drag you down with me. You understand that?"

"I don't really know what you mean."

"Can you imagine what it feels like to drown in a river of shit?"

"Not really."

"Well, I think you might be about to find out."

I hang up.

So it's official. Subnormal intelligence is clearly no longer a bar to becoming a university professor.

I should have gone into academia. I should have taken the easy path. It's not as if I'm lacking the modest count of marbles required. I could be eating crumpets in front of an open fire in an Oxford senior common room right now, watching London burn on the TV. Supervise the odd undergrad. Publish a book every five years or so. Vintage port on tap. What could possibly be nicer? Life could have been so easy.

I've always been too ambitious for my own good. I wanted to make the world a better place. Bloody idiotic waste of time. People are ungrateful bastards who hate you for trying to help them. That's what politics has taught me. In fact, that's a pretty good working title for my memoirs, right there. *People Are Ungrateful Bastards Who Hate You for Trying to Help Them* by Hugo Nelson. A surefire best seller. I could use it to launch a post-political career as a de-motivational speaker, traveling the world encouraging people not to work so hard, because it's all a waste of effort. Trouble is, only corporations could afford me, and they don't want to hear that stuff.

I'm beginning to sound like a Commie. Pull yourself together, Hugo. Get back on that horse. Fight the good fight. Crumpets and port can wait.

Stand up, walk out of your office, and make something happen.

A while ago, my son showed me a truly delicious video on YouTube. It is of a beach somewhere in America on which a whale has washed up, dead. The local police chief decides that the best way to dispose of the problem of the vast, rotting corpse is to blow it up, after which he believes the whale parts will simply wash out to sea. A crowd gathers. The explosives are laid. You can see the excitement on the faces of the crowd, until the explosives detonate, at which point everyone realizes this has been a huge mistake. Suddenly, nobody's having fun. Rotting whale meat rains down. That instantaneous shift from "fun day out" to "standing in a hail-storm of putrefying whale intestine" is genuinely hilarious.

I indulge myself with this brief *circumlocutio* as a means of illustrating my situation. At this moment, my career is that whale and Pyle is the police chief. He's already laid the charge. What I need to do is find a way to defuse those explosives before the rotting carcass of my career is blasted into the sky.

This metaphor doesn't make much sense, does it? My calling as a poet never quite got off the ground, probably for good reason.

I decide to go online and watch the video one more time. It'll cheer me up. When facing adversity, a positive frame of mind is crucial. A smile is the best starting point for...oh, shut up, Hugo, and do something useful.

Something useful.
A thing of use.
An action with a constructive outcome.
Hmm.

'I was embarrassed by my reading...I didn't feel good about myself. I got no pride in myself. I was angry over every single little thing. It didn't take a lot to set me off...so I think why not bunk school and go and do a bit of thieving?...Other people go from school to university. We go from school to prison...School shatters your dreams before you get anywhere.'

Harriet Sergeant, *Among The Hoods: Exposing the Truth About Britain's Gangs*

TROY

I'm out back through the folding doors where there's air. Just a small square of concrete—high walls all around—but look up and there's sky. Breathe in and it's fresh, or almost. Better than inside anyway. Middle of the day the whole place is so bright the whiteness slaps your eyeballs and the concrete's mostly too hot to sit on, but there's a corner in the shade, so I go there for a bit.

It's good to be alone and just think.

Place like this—probably the closest you get to outdoors when you're in jail. Even sweltering hot that's an idea makes me shiver. Ice down my spine.

Weird how it's nice to be on your own, then your mind goes down a turning and suddenly it ain't—so I'm glad when Femi comes out and sits next to me—but I can tell by the way he walks and the look on his face that he's edgy—and that even though he's acting like it's an accident, he's come to find me on purpose.

Don't speak. Just wait for him.

A'ight? he says.

I nod but so small it hardly even counts. I know what's coming, and I already ain't into it.

He leans in. *We got to get out,* he says. *This is crazy, man—you know a way out?*

Past the feds?

Yeah.

'Course I don't. I don't know where the feds are, do I?

He looks at me—desperate eyes—like he ain't drank for days and I'm a Coke.

You don't mean past the feds, do you? I say. *You know that ain't possible. You talking about going to the feds, ain't you?*

Anything, man, just anything! It's like he's shouting and whispering at the same time.

I know he's right. Logical thing is to save yourself—no doubt—just walk out the door and do whatever the feds say— blame it all on the others. That's what logic says. But there ain't one drop of my blood that'd let me do that. Not one.

Why? 'Cause of Blaze. Femi's saying lay it all on Blaze— and even if that's the truth—even if it was all him—that ain't something I can do.

The others is scared of him. Not me. That ain't why I wouldn't do it. With me and Blaze it's something different.

All these years I never actually seen him fight—throw a punch—at least not on one of our own, so there's no reason why he should have a rep or why anyone should be afraid of him. I mean, no reason that comes from facts—from something he's actually done. But nobody wants to be on his bad side.

I only seen him angry once or twice—maybe with the feds or with his mum—and you don't want to be on the receiving end of it because it's like a volcano, man, the power of it.

I'm the same, but I ain't got the size or the personality. I don't know what it is, but when I lose it people just look at me like I'm a freak, so I have to stay in control always—as much as I can—and it's hard, man, I tell you it's hard with the shit I got to go through. All my life people act like I'm wild or out of control or something, but they don't know nothing about what it's like—about the effort, man, the constant effort what I got to do to hold myself in—to keep walking that line. Yeah, I'm angry, but you would be, too—if you lived what I lived. Nobody ever said, *He done well, he got through a whole day putting up with everything without once losing his shit.* Nobody ever said that about me—they always just tell me what I done wrong.

People with cars and houses and jobs and money in their pocket—they don't know what it's like, they don't got a clue what it's like to get through even one day when everyone's against you and there's nothing for you except *don't go there—don't do this—don't say that—stay out of the way—just shut up and disappear*—they don't got a clue, man. They think I'm a freak, they think I'm a criminal, they think I got no self-control, they don't know nothing. I'm made of self-control, man—my blood is self-control—my heart just pumps self-control around my body, because if it didn't, I'd be running around killing people. That ain't a threat or nothing—I ain't crazy—I'm just saying you try getting on from day to day to day knowing you ain't never going to have nothing—ain't no job nowhere with your name on it and never will be. Cradle to grave, man, you think about it—what do you think that's like?

I'm not really into remembering shit—I mean, what's the point—looking back just messes with your head—but there's some things about Blaze you can't forget. When we was small we used to hang out at the playground—me, Blaze, Femi, Lee, and others sometimes—but mostly us four as a group the same age and everything. Most of it was smashed up and the slide had a hole in it halfway down and the merry-go-round didn't go around and everything was covered in graffiti and the ground was a kind of gravelly concrete that some guy invented especially as the best thing to grate skin off knees—but there was at least a climbing frame made of metal—solid, man, weren't no way to smash that up. Maybe it's because when you're a kid you're shorter than everyone else—I don't know—but as soon as there's something to go up—to make you higher—you just want to do it. So that's where we was—all weathers—up that climbing frame.

I was there the most—for obvious reasons, with Mum so messed up all the time—it wasn't safe to be home—you never knew if she'd be happy or out of it or crazy violent or what—I mean, from real small, I just knew I was better off somewhere else. Cold rain, whatever—I'd be on that climbing frame waiting to see who else would show. Maybe they'd take me back to their apartment—maybe I'd get fed that way—I tell you, I was hungry most of the time, crazy hungry—people don't believe me, but it's true. Apart from me, Blaze was there most often. His mum wasn't as bad as mine—she wasn't on anything—but there was a guy and another one after him in and out of the place that weren't good—and same as me, Blaze knew to just stay out the way, that's what's safest.

I ain't much protection to nobody. I mean, I'm small. Probably would have been anyway, but the shit Mum gave me to eat when she gave me anything—ain't hardly surprising I'm little. Anyway, what I'm saying is, me and Blaze, we looked after each other. Even if there ain't nobody out to fight you—even if there ain't no actual person threatening you—the difference between being alone and having someone else, it's like another world. It's the same as the difference between empty pockets and having cash.

Point is, them cold days when nobody wants to be out—when that playground's almost the shittest place in the world—them days it was just me and Blaze. Everyone else home in the warm—me and Blaze was out there—or maybe somewhere else looking for something to do—and I ain't talking once or twice, I'm saying day after day after day—just me and Blaze like brothers, man, more than brothers—I'm telling you, he saved my life and I know I ain't nothing compared to him, but I swear I saved his.

Blaze found places for us to go—I don't know how—and he never got lost, or if he did, he never let on, and we always found our way back eventually. He never been scared, Blaze—he ain't scared of nothing—I swear, if he'd been born somewhere else—if he'd had a proper family that looked out for him, he could have done anything. It's what sets him apart, it's what makes people follow him; it's like a force, a secret weapon or something—he just ain't afraid—don't even know what it means—it's like an energy, man, just a buzz to be around that and to see where it takes you.

I ain't no use in a fight and I ain't even got much mouth on me—can't get the right words out when I need them—but I got a role, 'cause fear's there for a reason, like sweat is and hunger is and pain is. Them things are there to tell you something, but it's a voice Blaze don't hear, so I'm his sensors—like antenna to spot things he don't see or hear or feel, and he always listens to me, 'cause he knows it. Whatever crazy shit is going on—I just got to look at him a certain way and he'll know what I mean—won't question me or nothing—he'll just know it's time to bail and we do. No question. Bang, we're gone.

In school Blaze never took any shit, neither, at least not from other kids. Even older ones knew he was somebody and left him alone—didn't have to prove it in a fight or nothing. Teachers were different, though. The same thing that protected him in the outside world—that I-ain't-afraid-of-you stare—made teachers hate him. It was like they could see straight away he didn't accept the rules—didn't accept that he was less than them and they could push him about—didn't accept that he had to respect them just 'cause they was at the front of the class with posh clothes and posh words and all that. He just wasn't playing that whole game and they didn't know what to do about it. Man, they *hated* him—he was their worst nightmare and he knew it, and he just didn't care.

School was a joke anyway—like a cross between a zoo and a prison to keep us off the streets until we was a bit older. From the minute you walked in on the first day, you could feel the pointlessness—teachers scurrying around either afraid or psycho angry or just waiting to get home, get another job, just get away. I remember whole lessons where the teacher would say, *I'm not starting till you're quiet—you have to stand up till you're quiet,* and we'd just stand there for the whole forty-five minutes with somebody somewhere shouting or acting up or messing around—and the whole lesson would go by just a total waste of time. The only way to make it not a waste of time was to join in the fooling around—at least that was fun.

Blaze wasn't the worst—neither was I—we was just bored and there was something about us the teachers hated. When they lost it and they needed someone to blame, it was always him or me—don't know why, they just didn't like the look of us. Ghetto eyes or something, I don't know. We weren't the worst.

Like I say, school was a joke. I'm not an idiot, I seen other schools on TV—kids sitting in rows listening, writing, learning stuff for their exams. If I'd been somewhere like that everything would be different, but people like me don't get a chance—don't even get taught to read and write proper—so after that, what chance you got—what chance of getting work and earning, what chance?

More than anyone Blaze knew from day one it was all pointless—but it was as if he had a secret plan—as if he always knew he'd climb out of the chaos and find his own path. We all knew he would, too, and we wanted to go with him.

But now it don't look like that's happening, 'cause here we are in this warehouse and I mean, it's exciting, but this ain't a way out and it ain't a way up. We always been trapped and now we trapped ourselves worse than ever and it's like water going around and around getting closer and closer to the drain faster and faster and that's that. Ain't no question where this is leading.

People always talk about good and bad, and I know we steal stuff and mess people up and we're like a proper menace—but that ain't half the story, 'cause I know Blaze and he knows me, and I swear to God, as far as I'm concerned Blaze is a saint—he's like my guardian angel, he's the only good person I ever known who'll step up to pull me out of the shit. It's like blood, man, that's how it is. He's the only one that's ever looked out for me.

I mean, there's Rose, too. There's always Rose. She was my foster mother after child services got onto my mum and took me away—I mean, Rose looked after me proper good and fed me and everything, but after that went wrong—I mean, nobody ever told me why they just took me away— she was kind of old and maybe I flipped out one too many times, I don't know—but I never knew that could happen. I never knew they'd take me away from Rose and I'd never see her again—nobody warned me or nothing—and after that, you know I was just too angry, man, I couldn't keep my shit together. After that I just kept on getting moved from place to place—nobody could take what I was like—maybe it's my fault, I don't know, but that's how I ended up in the hostel. No kitchen, nothing to eat, crazy messed-up people everywhere—I mean, there's a posh lobby so it looks all clean and nice when people step inside—the suits the politicians, them people—but the rooms, man, I swear it's the pits you wouldn't believe. So I'm just saying yeah, there was Rose. She was good to me. She was good. But that didn't last—the only one that's lasted is Blaze—he's always there for me and I'm always there for him.

Can't even tell if Blaze planned this or if it just happened. No difference anyway. 'Cause whatever it is I'm with him. He's blood. And if Femi thinks he can turn me, he don't know nothing about nothing.

Although some biological psychiatrists were puzzled by the fact that stimulants seemed paradoxically to calm hyperactive children, the belief in their effectiveness was such that, in some cases, stimulants were used as a diagnostic tool: if they calmed down an overactive, impulsive child, then the child likely had hyperactivity. More important for parents, however, was that stimulants were a quicker, easier and less expensive treatment modality than arranging for psychotherapy or analysing and attempting to change the social factors that might be contributing to such behaviour. Such drugs appeared to be veritable magic bullets...Stimulants did what psychotherapy could not do: they calmed children down within minutes.

Matthew Smith, *Hyperactive: The Controversial History of ADHD*

FEMI

Anything, man, just anything! I says, and I can hear the desperation in my voice 'cause I know time's running out, I know the feds could run in here any second, and I got to get out before then to show I'm different—to show I ain't into this.

And Troy just sits there, his face all blank almost like he's bored, like he's miles away. And I'm thinking, *What's wrong with you, man, can't you see we got to get out,* 'cause he ain't stupid, Troy, he knows what's what. I mean, I just need one person to go with me. I ain't got the balls to do it on my own, and I don't even know where to go—I mean, out the front door? Just like that? How do I know they won't gun me down? How do I know what they'll do to me? I need one other person to make it seem like the right thing, and it has to be

Troy—I mean, who else? Matchstick no way, and Lee's just a liability, and Karen, she knows the score—she's thinking about it—but I can't trust her. She'll say anything, do anything, to get what she wants; I ain't going nowhere with her. It's got to be Troy.

And he sits there just staring into space like he's almost forgotten we're talking. Then eventually he turns and looks at me and looks away and says, *That ain't going to happen.* He can't never look at you and speak at the same time. He's always looking down or away or something. Shifty, scared, I don't know what it is, but it's like there's something wrapped around him keeping him separate. He's always in his own place.

He don't have to say more, I can see on his face nothing'll change his mind. He's small, Troy—ain't nobody afraid of him—but there's ice in his voice when he says it that makes me worry.

Your choice, I says, all calm like I don't even care. He's looking up at the sky and I'm watching his face to see what he's thinking, but there ain't no clues.

Still casual, I says, *Don't tell Blaze what I said.*

Troy picks up a stone—chucks it at the zigzag door. *He knows.*

Just two words, but hearing them's like a shank going into me. Suddenly I ain't even got the breath to speak.

Troy chucks another stone. It clitter-clatters between the folds of metal before hitting the concrete. He's looking for the next stone, running a finger through the dirt, when he says, *He knows already. Don't trust you no more.*

How can he know? I only just said it. It's embarrassing, the voice on me. All high and squeaky.

He knows.

The more the schools have experience of docile, conformist children on medication, particularly in this performance league table obsessed and resource-stretched environment, the more schools are making their own diagnosis and suggesting medication to parents. It takes a very brave parent to follow their gut instinct, not to give their children psychiatric drugs and resist the growing tide of pressure. As for the children themselves, they are drowning in the discourse of disability and genetic inadequacy.

Sami Timimi, *Naughty Boys: Anti-Social Behaviour, ADHD and the Role of Culture*

THE JOURNALIST

I sometimes use an alias when I'm going off-road with my research: Judy Andrews. My theory is that it makes people subconsciously think of Mary Poppins without quite knowing why. When I'm Judy Andrews, people trust me; they tell me things they might not otherwise, and if they become suspicious I just hang up the phone and they can't find me.

I start with the school closest to the mayor's office. If there's going to be a scandal, that's a good place to set it.

"Hello, my name's Judy Andrews. I'm calling from the mayor's office. We're collating some statistics on uptake procedures for the Concentr8 program. Could I possibly have a word with the headmistress?"

Within a minute I'm through, and she's telling me everything. It all comes out. Like fishing, except instead of having to go out with a line, these fish jump out of the water, walk to your house, cook themselves, lie down on your plate, and hand you some cutlery. She gives me the whole story—how she was told that ten percent of pupils were eligible, and that it was expected to have a significantly beneficial effect on the behavior of the pupils selected for the program. Schools would be rated for their uptake ratios on future inspectors' reports. The closer to the full ten percent, the better.

The head chose the children, following discussion with teachers about difficult pupils, and parents were invited to the psychological assessments, during which the assistance available from the benefits system for those with an ADHD diagnosis was explained, and the necessary forms for participation in the program were signed.

"So it was your job to recommend people for the program?" I ask.

"With the help of the teachers, yes."

"And of those you put forward, do you have any idea what proportion joined the program?"

"Oh, almost all of them."

"Almost all? More than ninety percent?"

"Oh, closer to ninety-five. A few felt the diagnosis was some kind of stigma, which seemed like a real shame to us, because the benefit of these drugs is really crystal clear in terms of making a certain kind of child more cooperative in the classroom environment, but I think most people saw that the child benefits from the drug, the school benefits from improved behavior, society benefits from having less truancy, and the parent benefits from...well, the extra benefit."

"So the only people who turned it down were parents? The doctors agreed with your diagnosis in every case."

"I think so. I mean, we know our children very well."

"Well enough to diagnose mental illness?"

"We're not doctors, of course. I'd never dream to think I was *diagnosing* anything, I...er...where did you say you were calling from again?"

"That's all I need for now. Thank you so much for your time."

I hang up. I call ten more schools. It's the same story in every one. Troublesome kids picked out by teachers, put forward for the program, almost all of them ending up on the drug that keeps them quiet, while parents are kept happy with the reward of disability benefit. And as Pyle told me, this wasn't even a new policy, it was just the old policy, pushed harder, better funded, with a newer, cheaper drug.

But doctors going into schools rather than children being referred to doctors made the whole enterprise feel different. Was this really a child mental health program, or was it preemptive policing?

Of course, there's no answer to that question, certainly not an answer you'd ever get from a politician, but I now had enough material to ask the question. I had my scoop.

The story was too good for the weekend supplement, and it couldn't wait. This one would be for the next day's front page.

A 1970 story in the *Washington Post*, which revealed that up to 10 per cent of schoolchildren in Omaha, Nebraska were being prescribed behaviour-modifying drugs such as Ritalin, put a spotlight on such concerns and spurred Congressional hearings into the issue . . . It was claimed that African American students in Minneapolis were being especially singled out for drug treatment.

Matthew Smith, *Hyperactive: The Controversial History of ADHD*

KAREN

It's late when things kick off? I mean, maybe it's been brewing for a while and I didn't notice, but anyway, it's after we all eaten. More Nando's again courtesy of the feds. I can see Blaze is in the zone, 'cause he goes quiet and far away, but you don't know what he's planning 'cause you never do. He's in the big chair just sitting there eating, but it's like he can't even hear any of us.

Then he gets up, walks off, comes back with the massive wrench everyone was chucking around the night before. You can see the weight of it by the ripple in his forearms, the skin tight over his knuckles where he's gripping.

Let's do one-on-one, he says. Don't even know what he means, but everyone except Lee and me looks away 'cause there's suddenly a weird vibe.

He's staring down Femi.

Femi, he says. *Let's play.*

I'm eating, says Femi, not even looking up.

It's okay, I'll wait, says Blaze.

So Femi finishes his chicken and there's total silence except for the sound of his chewing. He's eating slower and slower.

I swear, I get a bit horny just watching? Don't judge me, but it's weird, that's the effect. I can see Blaze's chest going up and down, total focus in his eyes. Shiny arms under the sweat like polished wood. I don't know what it is he's going to do to Femi, but I swear there's an electricity crackling off him strong and hot.

Femi stands up and stares at Blaze. You can see he's made a decision. It's run or fight, and there ain't nowhere to run, so he's going to fight.

Play? he says, sort of trying to sneer but it don't really come out right.

You go that side, says Blaze. *First hit wins. Winner stays on.*

Femi goes opposite Blaze. Tries to stare him down, but by the way he's licking his lips, you can see the effort and the fear.

Ready? says Blaze.

Femi crouches. Nods.

Blaze chucks the wrench. Not straight, though, and Femi don't even have to dodge. But the weight and force of it is lethal. Me and Lee and Troy and Matchstick, we're all just frozen—can't hardly believe what's happening in front of us.

Femi gets the wrench and walks back. Aims. Blaze is loose and relaxed. Almost smiling.

Femi chucks. Not half the power, but a better aim. Blaze sways back like he's got all the time he needs, and it flies past his face. Close but harmless.

Same again. Second time Femi has to dodge. The wrench takes a chunk out of the wall behind him.

It's Blaze's fourth or fifth throw before there's contact. You can see him giving it everything and it's faster than the ones before. The wrench is going straight for Femi's head and there's a moment of panic on his face, 'cause you can see him thinking dodge-or-parry, dodge-or-parry, but he don't do neither and I swear, for a moment I think he might actually die, 'cause if that thing got you in the face, you really would? Then his arm comes up and there's this sick crunch when it hits him just under the elbow. It ain't even human, that noise, the sound of it almost makes you want to puke. He howls and falls to the floor holding his arm.

Blaze is the first to go over. He don't rush, but the rest of us, it's almost like we're glued to the floor or something.

You okay?

Femi only swears, but I suppose that means he's okay. If he weren't moving or speaking, that would be worse.

Winner stays on, says Blaze, looking at the other guys.

Nobody says nothing.

No expression on his face, Blaze turns away and walks up to the office, not fast, not slow, not even looking back.

At the top he drops the wrench off the balcony. The sound when it lands—steel on concrete—it's like a bullet going off. Creeps me out, so I don't know what it does to Femi.

I feel weird now? Don't want to go up there with him? All the boys are too chickenshit to go and help Femi, so it's me that does it. I go under his good side and lift him to the big chair. Sit him down and get water. Don't even care if Blaze sees, I really don't.

The injury ain't as bad as it sounded. I mean, he can still bend his arm. The fingers still move. Not even much of a bruise yet, but it'll come. He's going to have a purple elbow tomorrow.

It's ages before any of the others says anything, and it's Lee.

That was out of order, he says, real quiet. *Out of order.*

Troy don't say nothing.

You okay? says Matchstick.

Femi don't answer.

I don't go up. Just go for a wash at the sink, then bed down on the cardboard next to Femi. But I lay out a new spot for myself off to the side—don't want to be too close.

Troy takes some food in to the guy and I count off how long he's in there, but it ain't too long. He's looking at me when he comes out. He knows I'm watching him.

Ain't comfy on the floor, though—it's hard—so eventually I go up to the office where Blaze is. He's asleep when I go in, but just the sound of the door wakes him. I'm cold to him, like totally opposite from normal—'cause he got to know he gone too far with Femi—and I got my own thoughts, my own opinions, and that ain't right what he did. But I can't last out for long, I just can't. You don't need the details, but I swear, what happens next is something else—wild as it gets.

Day Four

To University of Iowa child psychiatrist Mark Stewart, children relying on Ritalin would have difficulty determining what their 'undrugged personality' was, as would their parents.

Matthew Smith, *Hyperactive: The Controversial History of ADHD*

TROY

I been following what they're saying about us on my phone. Papers, TV, radio, they're all mad for the hostage thing. Turns out the guy we got really is a bit of a nobody like he says, but that don't seem to make no difference to how much everyone loves the story. Basically we're famous, proper famous, apart from the fact that nobody knows who we are. Anonymously famous—which sounds impossible, like it don't mean anything, but it does. It's what I am now, and I tell you it ain't bad.

But this morning the buzz is different. Same thing repeated everywhere starting from one reporter who's done some story on Concentr8—and what they're saying is a headfuck. Not just 'cause it's like proper news—takes me ages to read the whole thing—figure out all the words—but when I make sense of it and it all comes together, it's mental. Everyone knows things kicked off because they stopped giving out Concentr8—but now it turns out they shouldn't have been dishing it out to us in the first place.

Everyone has always talked about it as medicine for a proper illness, but now it looks like they were giving it out to whoever. Just anyone they wanted to keep quiet, basically—people like me and Blaze and all of us in here.

119

And when you read this shit, you can't help thinking that with everything going mad on the streets, we was right to be angry—but we was angry about the wrong thing.

Me, I been on it since I was about eight, I reckon. Ages ago. It wasn't Concentr8 back then, it was something else. Me and Blaze was put on it at the same time. They was just hassling us at school constantly and things were bad at home—Mum a different person every time you walk in the apartment—just never knew who it would be waiting for you—then next thing I know I'm in the office of some doctor, a posh dick nagging me with a bunch of bullshit questions. Half the time he just talks over me to my mum on and on about my "behavior" and nobody asks about *her* behavior, nobody—'cause I got stories I could tell—mad stories that'd do your head in, but nobody's interested in that.

So then there's them pills. I mean, they tasted okay, so I just took them without even thinking about it. No big deal. Don't even know if I felt any different, it was such a long time ago—but people got off my back, left me alone more—I remember that. I wasn't in trouble so much. I had less energy for messing around, which everyone seemed pleased by. It was like being a bit sleepy all the time, just kind of calmer. The buzz that sets you off with ideas for bad shit to do—you know, ideas for stuff that no one's expecting, just naughty, funny, wild stuff, fun stuff—that buzzy voice went quiet, which was sort of a shame, but at least people got off my case. It felt okay to kind of daydream through lessons instead of just being so bored I had to act up and make something happen. Blaze was the same.

Back then they was only giving it to the really bad kids. It was more recent that they switched to Concentr8 and started giving it out left, right, and center. They swapped me over and said there'd be less side effects—which is kind of weird, since nobody ever said anything about side effects before turning up one day and telling me I'd have less of them if I changed—but I mean, everyone else was taking it, so it didn't feel like nothing to just switch over. I mean, it was medicine. Since when is medicine bad for you? That's like saying here's some food that'll make you hungry. I took it, everyone took it—didn't even cross my mind to say no.

Then when the policy changed and suddenly there wasn't no more Concentr8 to go around and it all just stopped—that was weird, man. I didn't think about it then, but if I go back to the week the pills ended, it was like plugging into something—like waking up when you didn't even know you was asleep—things popping brighter, clearer—normal but not normal, just kind of different, you know? I couldn't even tell if that was things going back to how they were before—'cause I been on it so long I can't remember what before was like. I was just a kid then, so how am I supposed to know?

There was kind of a new energy—and I didn't know it was going to turn into the riots or anything—but I could feel something was up. We was all coming off this drug— but the vibe was more like suddenly everyone was on something. The people who make them pills know what they're doing, 'cause I could feel the badness in me waking up—coming out of hibernation like it had been asleep for years—this wild dog inside me, and it was twitching and moving again—almost scary, but actually it felt good, man, real good. Like you're walking and walking and it's all you ever done, then suddenly you think, *What if I run—I haven't done that for ages*—and suddenly you're running and it's been so long you've forgotten what it feels like, but when those legs start moving fast and your blood starts pumping, you just never want to walk again—you want to run and run.

There's good dogs who are fat and sleepy and loll about all day—then there's bad dogs who howl and bite and chase—and that's who I am—it's in my bones or something—and when the bad dog in me wakes up again, I just know it's me coming back—and even though crazy things are going to happen, it's awesome, it's sweet, it's a door opening to I don't know what—I just know I got to go in and find out.

We was getting wilder 'cause we was angry they'd taken away the Concentr8—but this is weeks ago, man, and I can see now I didn't get the point—'cause it's only now reading that story on my phone that I realize what was making us angry was just that we was waking up again.

I didn't know it when the boxes of Concentr8 came into the warehouse delivered with our order of Nando's. Everyone piled in on the stuff and we all took it and there was like a massive party 'cause this is what we'd been fighting for and it was like we'd won. Taking them pills was our victory and we was happy—it was cool. And when everyone kind of chilled out and the atmosphere went down, I just thought that's normal; I mean, you win and you party and then you chill, that's the natural pattern.

Except now the whole place feels different—kind of slow and heavy, like one minute anything's possible, then suddenly just getting out of a chair feels like too much effort, you know? You can feel the downer in the air 'cause there's doubts creeping in. Nobody says anything, but it's in the air without words or nothing. We all know—Femi does—Karen does—I reckon even Lee, and he's slow, man, really slow—we all know where this is going.

After getting them pills there's no victory we can look for—nothing else to aim at—just killing time until they come in and get us. Only question is how long we can hold out before reality bursts in and we got to face the consequences of what we done—'cause this ain't no little thing—they're going to come down hard, man, hard. We rode the line right to the end now—can't go no further than this.

Everyone got a future—some more than others maybe—I never think about it usually, 'cause what's the point, it's just depressing—but right now it's like there's a brick wall right in front of us and you don't want to see what's over it—you don't want to look or even think about it—you just got to keep on running, knowing that any minute it's going to slam into you. There's a world of pain over that wall, but there ain't no turning around—we just got to keep on running toward it and through it and out the other side. This is the finish, man—the end of everything I know. I mean, there ain't much I'm leaving behind—can't think of nothing—but what's next has to be worse, don't it? There ain't going to be no mercy, nothing—just vengeance. They hate us more than anything and now they can do something about it. We're going to be the poster boys for all the badness across the whole city—everything, it's all going to come down on us. We're the famous ones now—not all them hundreds of others out on the streets stealing stuff— so it's going to be us paying the price for what they done—even though we ain't stole nothing. All the revenge that's been held in—building up—it's going to flare out, and it's got to strike some-where and it's going to be on us.

To the feds we're like a massive box of chocolates now—and they're just drooling, waiting to tuck into us and have a feast, man—a feast they always wanted.

We stole a box once years ago—me and Blaze—really posh ones with a purple ribbon around them and everything—ate the whole lot in one go, hiding behind some bins—split them fifty-fifty, it was amazing. Each one in its own little plastic hole the exact right size—every one a different shape, a different taste—hard ones, soft ones, gooey ones, fruity ones; the works. Sheet of puffy paper between the layers to keep them all comfy and perfect. After they was all gone we found a leaflet with little pictures saying what was in each one—couldn't read half of it but kept it anyway in my pocket for like a week or something—took it out, looked at the pictures again and again till I lost it.

Ain't good to look back, neither—even happy things like that make you sad remembering them—don't know why.

That news story, I only show it to Blaze. The others is always doing stuff on their phones, so they must have seen some version of it—'cause it's everywhere—but they don't seem that bothered. They don't get it. Blaze, I don't know what he seen, 'cause he's up in the office most of the time with Karen. It's just unbelievable how much they're at it—on and on like rabbits—I mean, I don't know nothing about rabbits, ain't never even seen one, but that's what they say, ain't it? For when you can't get enough?

I can't get enough, neither—but in the other sense, as in like I can't get *none*. I ain't got the talk, ain't got the looks, ain't got no money, nothing. Whatever else goes bad for Blaze, at least he got that. If I had that, don't reckon any of the rest of it would bother me—but I'll get my chance eventually; it's got to happen someday and I'm telling you I'll be ready—I'll treat my woman good, so good she'll keep me forever. Maybe not forever, but you know—a long time.

You'd think Blaze would be interested in what's going on out there—what they're saying about us—but the thing about Blaze, the most important thing, is that he never cares what nobody says about him or thinks.

When he comes down with that sleepy just-done-it smile on his face, I show him my phone and he don't say nothing—but he reads it twice slowly—not as slow as me, but careful—stopping to figure every word—and I can see on his face he gets it straightaway—and he knows it changes everything just like I do.

He looks at me but he still don't speak—just goes off on his own for a while and Karen tries to go with him, but he shrugs her off and she stares at me all pissed off, like she thinks it's my fault—like it's something to do with me and her—something personal, like bitchy gossip or something—she's such a dick, don't understand nothing.

He comes back, just quietly slips in again—and we're all hanging out like normal, but I sense that he's made a decision and when the time's right, he's going to say something—and I know that when he does, everyone except me is going to be all *What the fuck?!*

But he don't say nothing—not at first. Then after lunch, when everyone takes a pill, I watch him and I can see he knows I'm watching, and when the packet comes to him, he just passes it on. Don't take one. He does it real quiet so nobody says anything or even notices, but I don't take my eyes off him for a second and I know he skips it. He don't look at me for a few seconds—maybe five or six; it's weird I'm counting them off in my head, don't know why—then when he does he sees me looking at him and he knows I've noticed. I give him a nod and he knows what I mean. *Me too,* I'm saying, and just by the way he blinks slow and heavy, I can see that he's with me—that neither of us is going to take that stuff again.

Like I said, he's blood—half the time we don't even need to speak; we can talk without words. Best way, too, 'cause words ain't my thing, don't come natural to me. Never have. Can't get out my mouth what's in my head. I ain't thick, not like Lee—just 'cause you can't talk good don't mean you're thick. Lee's different. I mean he's proper slow—you can tell by how his mouth hangs half-open like a dog's. I swear to God, you stick a pin in Lee's head, it'd just go pop—ain't nothing in there except a cloud of puff.

They think they got us surrounded, but they ain't. Can't go out the way we got in, 'cause that's where the feds is—but Matchstick knows a way jigging through a hole in the wall from this warehouse into another one, then down some alleys or something to a hole in the railway fence. He goes out every day—gets us stuff we need—buys it, steals it, whatever. Just him and Blaze know the way. If the others knew they might run for it, so it's kind of a secret. Me, I don't even care, 'cause I ain't going nowhere.

Their mum will be mad angry, 'cause she's given up on Blaze, but she still got hopes for Matchstick—he's a good kid and he's smart, but he thinks Blaze is God, so basically she don't stand a chance—which drives her mental. Matchstick tangled up in what's going on out here—that'll send her ballistic, I swear. Blaze is her own son, but if she weren't afraid of him I reckon she'd want to kill him sometimes—as in literally kill him. Stealing and robbing's bad enough, but this is a whole other level, and Matchstick's just a kid—it ain't right for him to be involved—but he is now, so that's that. Same for all of us. Happened so fast I feel like nobody actually chose to do it except Blaze, but there's no way back now.

He don't say much, Matchstick—same as his brother—but he's quick and he can climb anything like he got spider feet, so ain't nothing can stop him going nowhere, least of all his mum. He's going to be a serious rascal when he's big, but for now he's our messenger—our eyes and ears, a kind of human periscope—which is what they use to see out of submarines. I'm telling you, I ain't thick; I watch history channels and I don't forget nothing. I got tons of shit in my head you wouldn't believe was in there, but it is.

It's like Matchstick is invisible, the way he can float in and out of places without anyone noticing, and it ain't just 'cause he's small. It's a state of mind—like a Zen thing—like he can do something that just makes people look through him. I tell him to get us a newspaper—a proper one, old-school, on paper—the one that started the story. I give him the money for it and everything. I know he could steal one no trouble, but it don't seem worth the risk—not today—'cause I need that paper, I need him to come back with the paper. I can't trust the hostage with my phone. He could call someone. He could threaten to smash it. I don't trust nobody with my phone to be honest, but I want him to see the story—tell me what he knows—explain it and stuff. Ain't like he'll say no, is it? Ain't like he got something better to do.

So when Matchstick gets back, I go straight in with some food and the newspaper. He reads it with his eyes dancing back and forward over the page, almost gulping down the words like he's as hungry for that as he is for food. Makes me feel sorry for him almost. It's a glimpse through the front, the I-ain't-scared act. He never lets me see he's afraid or desperate—at least he tries to hide it—and he's almost good enough for it to be convincing. But watching him read, I feel like I can see behind the act. I suppose it's the first time I ever been in with him when he's been doing anything other than looking up at me—shitting bricks—wondering what I'm going to do to him.

His face ain't doing nothing—he don't look happy or sad or anything else that you could put a word to—but while he's looking down reading the paper, I feel like I can see for the first time who he is and how much he wants to get home. He ain't only the guy tied to the radiator—he's a person with a life before he got here, and a life after we let him go, and this is just like an episode for him. But he don't know that—not for sure. He thinks it might be the end. He don't know me, he don't know Blaze, he don't know what we want—for all he can tell, we're proper killers. We dragged him here and tied him up. He got no idea what we'll do next—*we* got no idea what we'll do next—but the difference is, he don't know what our limits are. He don't know if he'll even get out alive. I could tell him, I suppose, but it don't feel right—I mean, Blaze is in charge; it just ain't my place. And even though I get Blaze better than anyone—these last few days I been wondering how much I really know—I mean, do I really got any idea where he'll stop? I always thought I did, but now I ain't sure.

You know anything about this? I say when he looks up from the paper.

No! It's not my department! I've got nothing to do with it!

I ain't threatening you. I'm just asking. You reckon it's true?

I can see his brain whirring, trying to figure what's safest to say.

Just tell me the truth. I'm asking your opinion, ain't nothing else.
Why?
'Cause you work there. You know stuff.
Not much.
More than I know.
Why do you care what I think? he says almost angrily. It's cornered dogs that bite—I mean, I know he can't do anything all tied up, but I can see he's panicking like he could flip—and when you flip, you'll do crazy shit.

I sit down so I'm on the same level as him—close but not too close. Don't want him lashing out or nothing. Lower my voice and speak all gentle like what we got is a secret. *I thought you said we could help each other.*

I see boy after boy who has been diagnosed and medicated for years coming to my clinics. I see boy after boy who hates taking these medicines. I discuss the controversies with the parents and nearly all want to subsequently reduce the dose or bring their children off the tablets. I have seen boy after boy come off stimulants. Parents tell me children started eating normally again, put on weight, came out of their shell and began to express themselves. They were transformed.

Sami Timimi, *Naughty Boys: Anti-Social Behaviour, ADHD and the Role of Culture*

THE HOSTAGE

I keep on thinking about that phone, crushed, on a sidewalk near my office. I wonder if it is still functional enough to ring. I wonder who's been ringing it. My roommates, I hope—to ask where I am—unless they've assumed I'm on a trip I happened never to mention. There's no particular reason why my absence from the apartment should alarm them. My parents—maybe—but it's not as if the lack of an answer or callback would lead them to assume anything is wrong. Carla—possible, but unlikely. That phase of post-breakup heart-to-hearts has passed. It's a month or more between calls now. Her voice each time a little more distant, a little less interested. She has a new boyfriend, I'm sure of it. I daren't ask, and she hasn't said anything, but I can tell. It's there in the lilt of her speech, in the speed of her hang-up. The ongoing conversations were an insurance policy she no longer needs. The last, frail bond between us has snapped.

I can spend hours wondering who it was that alerted the police. I can spend hours wondering why they haven't charged in and rescued me. I can spend hours thinking nothing at all. Then again, perhaps these hours are actually minutes. It's impossible to tell. I am physically tied down, but my mind is absolutely adrift—detached from every marker that gets you through a day. This, perhaps, is what shipwreck feels like. I am a landlocked castaway.

I'm more afraid and less afraid, now. More afraid of the situation—of how this has gone on so long, got so strange, that any outcome now seems possible—but less afraid of the kids. I've got it straight who each of them is, and it's only Blaze who really frightens me. The others don't seem to have much more idea of what's going on than I do.

It's not safe to ignore them when they come in, but it's best to keep them away, so my strategy now is to bore them—to do as little as possible. The only one I talk to is the one who brings me food. I've given up on trying to hatch any kind of plan with him, but it seems like a good idea to keep him on my side—to make sure there is one other person in the building who recognizes that I'm a human being.

At least I think I've given up, until he goes into a crouch, sits closer to me than he has ever sat, and whispers, "I thought you said we could help each other."

I've never felt so tired in my life. Never experienced such heaviness in my limbs and head. I feel semi-detached from my own thoughts now, as if the signals sent from my brain have become sluggish and dull. But for the first time in days, the sound of these words jolts me, wakes me up.

"Of course we can," I say. "If you can get me out of here, it changes everything for you."

"That ain't what I'm talking about," he says.

"What, then?"

He goes still. A lost look creeps across his face. He's at that strange age: part adult, part child. At this moment, he looks like a child.

"I'm looking after you, ain't I?" he says.

He's treading water. Building up to something.

"Barely. I've stayed in better hotels," I say. He lets out a snort that's halfway to a laugh. If he wants to slow down, that's fine. I need to show him he has all the time he needs. If he wants to chat, we can chat. I just need to keep him talking, keep him relaxed, let him say his piece when he's ready.

"I ain't never stayed in a hotel in my life, so maybe you're lucky."

"Right now, lucky isn't what I feel."

"What's it like?" he says. "In a hotel?"

I try not to show my surprise at his bizarre question. I can't understand why he's asking something so banal, but I need to keep the conversation flowing—though I'm so taken aback and foggy-headed, I can't think of an answer.

"The rooms?" he persists. "What's in the rooms, what do you get? Is it like all luxy? 'Cause people pays tons, don't they—what's in there that's so good?"

I'm baffled now, wondering if he's making fun of me in some way I can't quite understand. But then, so what if he is? I can't risk showing any scorn or disrespect.

"Well, it depends on the hotel," I reply cautiously.

"A posh one."

"Well, even in a really posh one—"

"How much?"

"What?"

"How much is a really posh one? The poshest one."

"I don't know. A top hotel in the middle of London? I don't know. Three, four hundred a night."

"FOUR HUNDRED?"

"Or more for a fancy suite or something."

"MORE? What's in there, what's in there?"

"Well, I've never been in a really fancy one, but I suppose it's still just a bed, a TV, nice chairs, room service."

"Where they bring you shit?"

"Yes." This is the closest I've come to smiling for days, but I force the muscles of my face into neutral.

"Anything? You just pick up the phone, they bring you anything?"

"Within reason. You have to pay for it."

"How much?"

"It depends what you ask for."

"What's the best one you been in, the most expensive?"

"The most expensive hotel I've been in?"

"Yeah."

"Why do you want to know?"

"I'm interested, ain't I?"

"Well...a couple of years ago I splurged. You really want to hear this?"

"Yeah, man."

"With a girlfriend. We had a holiday in the Maldives."

"What's the Maldives?"

"It's a chain of islands in the Indian Ocean. Tropical islands."

"Tropical? Like the pictures? Palm trees, white sand, all that stuff?"

"Yes. Sea so clear you can stand in it up to your neck and still see your toes."

"You went in it?"

"Of course. Every day."

"Every day? Shit! In the sea!"

"Have you never been in the sea?"

"No way, man. Wouldn't touch it."

"Why not?"

"Never seen it, but I seen the river, and it's disgusting."

"It's not like that. It's nice. Maybe one day you can save up and go somewhere hot and you could try it."

"You're dreaming, man."

"It's possible. Anything's possible. We've just got to get ourselves out of where we are now without anyone getting hurt."

"You got no idea, man."

"It's something to aim for, isn't it?"

"Forget it—you think that's an option, you don't know nothing."

There's a new look in his eye, as if a switch has been flicked. The anger that always seems to be just under the surface is suddenly an instant away from exploding out.

"Maybe I don't. I'm sorry," I say, not too craven, not frightened, just slowly backtracking.

He slaps the newspaper down on the floor between us. "So is this shit true?" he says.

"Seems like it."

"They was picking us out and drugging us up? Shutting up the difficult ones?"

"Looks like they've been doing it for years."

"Telling us they was helping us when actually they was helping themselves?"

"That's one way of looking at it. Should I be telling you it's all lies? Because it's not really in my interest to make you any angrier, is it?"

"I ain't angry with you."

I hold out the cord that's tying my hands. "Well, if this is what you do to your friends..."

"You ain't my friend, neither. I never said you was my friend," he snaps.

There's something gratifying in the way he has to deny this so vehemently. Maybe, just maybe, I'm reeling him in. At one of the high windows I see the diagonal blue streak of a police light. This glimpse sparks a surge in my pulse, but I look away fast. I don't want him to notice what I've seen.

"How long have you been on it?" I say.

"Couple of years. Then before that I was on something else did the same job. Can't remember how long."

"Why do you think they gave it to you?"

"Teachers always hated me. I'm not one of them kids just sits there and does what he's told—I just ain't. Never knew there was side effects. They told me I was ill and I had to take the stuff—said it was medicine and would make me better. Nobody asked me about it—what was I supposed to do? It was medicine. I didn't know my own mum was making money out of it. Should have figured it out—only time she ever took an interest."

"So if you don't want the pills anymore, and you took me hostage because of Concentr8 being taken away, maybe you should let me go."

It's a long shot, but I have to say it. I try to smile, keep it light, act as if I'm joking.

"Maybe I should. But it ain't up to me."

"Who is it up to?"

"Who d'you think?"

"I thought you said nobody was in charge."

He stands up, his face revealing another one of those dizzying shifts in mood. "Don't fuck with me," he says, spitting the words at me, before turning on his heel and walking out.

Doctors have a huge influence and power to turn our social and cultural expectations for children's behaviour into medical definitions of physical health, with those who do not conform to our social and cultural expectations being labelled as medically dysfunctional in some manner...Despite the volume of research and publications there is still no good evidence that supports the conclusion that ADHD is a medical disorder or that drug treatment is safe and effective.

Sami Timimi, *Naughty Boys: Anti-Social Behaviour, ADHD and the Role of Culture*

TROY

He was getting cheeky—trying his luck—so I tell him not to fuck with me and walk out thinking someone's going to be watching, but nobody's there. The whole warehouse is empty. I stop just outside the door and look around, then I notice a weird noise and a smell of, I don't know, smoke or something.

I go to the outdoors bit where it's walled in and sort of carpeted with about ten thousand cigarette butts and that's where I find everyone standing around a fire. Orange flames jiggling and swirling around an office chair—two big squares of slatted wood I ain't seen before—the drawers out of a desk somewhere—cardboard folders all curled and black. Lee turns up carrying a computer screen—a big old bulky one—and chucks it on the fire all proud like, *Look what I done!* and you can see he's kind of disappointed when it just squashes down the fire and don't catch. I reckon he thought it would explode or something.

Must be hard being Lee, 'cause everything that happens is a surprise, literally everything. If it had exploded, it might have killed one of us, and that would have been a surprise, too—but he obviously didn't think of that, neither.

Blaze is next to the fire holding a pile of medicine packets. Looks like he got all of them—all the Concentr8. One by one, calm as you like, he tosses them onto the fire.

Everyone else is standing back from him, just staring like they think he's gone crazy, but so crazy they're too afraid to jump in and stop him—'cause it ain't a good idea to get in Blaze's way when he's got this look in his eye. Nobody's saying nothing—they're frozen by the madness of what's happening 'cause they have no idea what's going on. I do—I get it straightaway; it's typical Blaze—he always waits and thinks, but when he makes his move it's extreme, man, he just does what needs to be done—no discussion, no dithering, no nothing.

The packets twist in on themselves—pimpling up, then blackening from the edges as they're swallowed up. Above each one for a second or two the flame burns green and I look around and everyone else is confused and freaked, but I feel this weird squelch in my heart, 'cause he just don't take no shit from nobody. He always knows what to do. There won't ever be another person like him. He never persuades nobody, not with words—he just does stuff and you got to follow him—no choice—'cause he's always in front and he just knows which way to go. Nobody can guess what he's thinking, not ever, but I'm closest. Everyone else is nowhere.

After the last one goes on the fire, Blaze don't even stay to watch it burn—he just walks out—not saying nothing—back into the warehouse. I watch him stroll in through the big folding door and sit on the armchair. He don't look up at me—he don't look at nobody—and there's an expression on his face that's sort of like a smile but also like something else completely. It's the way he sits—totally still—his arms not crossed, not on his lap, but laid out along the armrests—kind of relaxed but solid, like he's made of concrete—like he's a monument to something, but I don't know what. There's a vibe coming off him that makes me think this ain't the end of something, it's the beginning— almost like he's a boxer and there's ten thousand people watching and there's cheering and flashbulbs and shouting and the bell for the first round is about to go and in the middle of it all there's just a guy—motionless and quiet— knowing he's about to fight but not even afraid. He's in the zone—I can see it—but any moment it's all going to kick off and I don't know what he's going to do, but it's something big.

I look back at the others and there's the same thing on all their faces. *The fuck? Did he just . . . ?*

I got no desire to explain and I almost want to laugh at them, 'cause they don't understand nothing—but I keep it so nobody can see what I'm thinking.

Karen stares at me like it's my fault—like I done something to Blaze—but she knows nobody can't say nothing to make him change from what he's going to do anyway. She thinks it's me 'cause she wants to hate me—and she knows Blaze respects me the way he don't respect her. That makes her crazy jealous, and you know what? I like it.

I don't blink or nothing, I just let her stare at me and make her look away first. She's fit, though—she is so fit, man, it makes your nuts ache just being looked at by her. Madness, really, a girl as fine as that being jealous of me, but I reckon that's what makes her so mad, 'cause she knows I'm not a player—she thinks I'm nothing and maybe she's right, but she just can't get her head around me having something over her—it don't make no sense in her head—it's like an itch she can't scratch—like some shitty ringtone on and on and on and you'd think you'd just be able to cut it off, but you can't, because I ain't going nowhere. If Blaze wasn't Blaze she wouldn't put up with it, but Blaze is Blaze, so that's that—she can't do nothing.

Nobody figures what Blaze is doing with me, why he don't just get rid of me. Nobody gets it. Sometimes I don't even get it, but I know he won't drop me. Whatever happens—whatever anyone says or thinks, him and me are in it for good—we just are—we're blood, and Karen and everyone else will just have to deal. You can't trust no one in this life, just one person or maybe two if you're really lucky, and I got Blaze and he got me.

There were many other concerns about the drug. Its association with illicit amphetamines, known vernacularly as speed, bennies, uppers, crank or crystal, was particularly damaging, and contributed to the banning of Ritalin in Sweden during the late 1960s.

Matthew Smith, *Hyperactive: The Controversial History of ADHD*

FEMI

Burns it! The whole lot! Just like that—doesn't ask nobody, doesn't tell nobody, just chucks it on the fire like it's garbage and burns every packet. After everything we done to get the stuff! I swear, he's totally lost it, he's out of control, he's a maniac and we're stuck here in his little...I don't know what it is...it ain't a gang. I ain't in his gang. I ain't nothing to do with him—he ain't in charge of me. Strutting around like he's some gangster boss and we're his soldiers or slaves or whatever. No way! I didn't ask for that. I ain't into that.

And the others, they just take it! Nobody says nothing! Shit, it's like he's got them all tucked in his pocket.

It's true I don't say nothing, neither, but that don't mean I'm not thinking, not planning something, 'cause I ain't nobody's servant, not even Blaze's. I tried Troy, and he's shoulder to shoulder with him. Can't even get him to see what's totally obvious about the hole Blaze dug us into. Karen, neither; I mean, she's his girlfriend, ain't she, and she has moments when she sees he's lost it, but then she flips back and she's with him again. I mean, even if we talked, and she said I was right, I wouldn't know if five minutes later she'd change her mind again. Lee you can't even talk to proper, can't risk anything with him. Which just leaves Matchstick, and there's no way you can come between him and his brother, 'cause Blaze is like a god to him, but that don't mean he can't be useful, 'cause I got an idea. I got a plan. Last chance. I ain't walking out the front door on my own into all them feds, it's got to be something else, and this is it. This is the last thing I can think of.

So Blaze wanders off after burning the pills and the others stare at the fire like it's some funeral or cremation or something, but after it dies down they drift off, too, and I watch Matchstick, and when he's on his own I go up to him. Tell him I got two quid. Tell him I'm desperate for chocolate, like dying for it, and if he goes and gets me a Mars he can buy one for himself. He just says maybe, but he takes the money.

So I go up to the balcony and act like I'm chilling, but I'm not, I'm watching Matchstick, watching everywhere he goes, and it takes a while but eventually there's a moment when he looks up and nods to me and I know he's going to do it. I nod back just casual, like I ain't going anywhere, but the second he turns away I go after him. Close enough to follow, far enough away for him not to hear.

First off he's out through the folding door, and by the time I get there I've almost lost him, but I just see a flash of sneaker disappearing through a wall. Not like a ghost or nothing; I mean, there's a sheet of metal that bends upward and he goes through the gap, so I do too.

It's another warehouse no different from ours, and he crosses it, then goes up one of them rickety iron staircases to a balcony, same as next door, but this one's rusted like it might just fall off and crash down, and I mean, that would kill you, but that's where he goes, so I got to follow. 'Cause once I got Matchstick's secret way out, I'm free, ain't I?

Hard to keep quiet in these huge echoey spaces—stairs and balcony going *boom boom boom* under Matchstick's feet even though he don't hardly weigh nothing—but I do my best and he don't look back, don't seem to hear me or spot me. His steps are making a noise and with all the reverb, that probably blots out mine, and I'm almost going on tiptoes. Anyway, he got no idea I'm behind him, so maybe that's why he don't hear nothing.

Far end of the balcony he goes up on the edge railings and swings off a metal joist onto this long, narrow windowsill. He's out along the far wall now, no balcony underneath him, just a drop as tall as a house and he's edging along this sill and I'm just stuck to the spot thinking, *No way, man, what's he doing?* But then he gets to a broken window and crawls out. Onto the roof, it must be.

Shit, I don't like this, I mean, Matchstick can climb anything—it's his thing—it's like he's got superglue hands, but I ain't like that. What else is there, though? Go back?

Unreal, man, how I got into this. Never wanted to hurt nobody or break no laws or nothing, now here I am, got to be Mr. Olympic Gymnastics if I want to just get home and save my skin. So unfair. And my heart's zipping now like a hundred plus bpm, and there's the beginning of a pukey sickness swirling in my stomach, and it's just too much, it ain't what I deserve for what I done, which is basically nothing. All I done is watch other people do stuff. That's it. But if I get caught, nobody's going to believe that.

So I breathe and I think and I try and work out what's for the best, but my brain's useless now, just a mess of panic and freaking out, so then I just think, fuck it if Matchstick can climb out there, so can I.

Down to the end of the balcony. Up on the railing. Two hands on the roof joist. Try not to look down but then I do, and that floor, it's just so far away the only thing I can think about is how my brains will splat everywhere like a tomato if I fall. I swing and I get my legs up on the windowsill, but that's when I realize Matchstick must have timed it different, 'cause I got my feet on the sill but my hands is still gripping the joist and I'm at this stupid angle, almost horizontal—not standing, not hanging, just stuck. Wrists going weak already, ain't got long to figure this out, so I let my feet drop and take a swing. I get higher up this time onto the windowsill and let go with my hands, and this is the moment where if I get it wrong I'm dead.

So then I'm crouched on the sill heaving puff after puff of air into my lungs, and my eyes are shut and I'm thinking, *In a second I'm going to open my eyes to find out if I died or not*, then I realize if I'm thinking this I got to be alive, so I open my eyes and I am.

Ain't time to be grateful, 'cause Matchstick's getting away and it's a narrow ledge half-rotten, don't want to be up here any longer than I have to. So I crawl along—bits of wood crumbling and splintering under my knees—then out through the window and there's a good ledge to stand on. I mean, if I hadn't just been on that sill this would have freaked me out, 'cause there's another massive drop down to some parking lot, but it's as wide as a paving stone and I mean, it's not like you just fall off a paving stone for no reason, so I figure I'm pretty safe up here.

Can't see Matchstick, but there's only one way you can go to a turning at the edge of the roof. That must be where he's gone, and after that corner there must be a way down.

Don't know whether to go straight after him or take a moment. Suck in the freedom. 'Cause up above me is the sky—a huge unbroken slab of it all around—and I ain't seen that much space and air for ages. Spread out below is the city—apartment buildings, warehouses, railway lines, even a few trees. And blowing onto my face there's just the most beautiful thing of all, what I haven't felt for days. Wind. Not much, but enough to cool my face. Never would have thought anything that small or normal could feel so sweet.

Takes a while to get back to myself. Pulse, sweat, buzzy head, all that stuff, but I go a bit more normal in a minute or two, and walk on down the ledge to where Matchstick must have gone. Freedom, man—it's just the best feeling.

I go around the corner of the roof, and right in my face—straight in front of me—there's Blaze. Standing on the ledge so close we're almost nose to nose. The fright of it almost freezes me solid in one moment. I reel back, and I swear that would have been it if Blaze hadn't grabbed my arm and pulled me back in.

My legs are jelly now with the double shock of Blaze and then of almost falling off the roof, so I ain't got no pride left now, I just go down on my knees like a baby and breathe and breathe, but however much air I pull into me it never feels like enough, and I just feel like I'm suffocating. I can hear the stupid noises coming out of my mouth like choking, sobbing, I don't know what it is, and I ain't even got it in me to feel embarrassed.

All I can see is the concrete and Blaze's sneakers. Then he sits next to me with his legs dangling down off the edge like there ain't even no drop.

What up? he says, not sounding angry or nothing, but there's a weirdness in the not-angry voice that sounds even more psycho than if he was laying into me.

I'm sorry Blaze, I'm sorry, I say, blubbing the words out all wobbly and spitty and feeble.

Where you going?

I don't know.

Matchstick is there right behind him. Nothing in his eyes, just nothing.

Why's you following my brother?

I don't know, I'm sorry, I just wanted some chocolate.

Don't lie to me, man. Don't lie to me.

There's a long silence but I don't know how long, 'cause I'm either sinking or floating or something, I just don't hardly know who I am or where I am no more. Eventually without even choosing what to say, the truth—or half of it—comes out my mouth in a big gush. *You burned our pills! It's done my head in! That's my medicine! I need it and we fought for it, we all fought for it together, then you didn't say nothing and you just burned it, man, you burned it! That ain't fair. You should have said! You should... I don't know... it ain't fair, that's my medicine! I need it!*

Then it's quiet again—so quiet I can hear the wind. Must be a loose cable up here, 'cause I can hear a *clack clack clack* from up on the roof behind us. Or maybe it's a bird, I don't know.

You need it? says Blaze, eventually. His voice sounds almost kind, but I can't trust it. There has to be something else hidden behind it, I don't know what.

Yeah! I need it. Doctors said I do and I do. But you burned it for no reason!

You want some?

'Course I do!

Well, that's all you needed to say.

What? I say.

Don't need to lie and cheat and sneak about. Tricking my little brother. You just need to come to me.

But you burned it!

Some of it. Kept a few back, didn't I? Just in case. You want some?

Yeah.

You should have just asked me that in the first place, shouldn't you?

I'm sorry.

You want it now?

Yeah.

Well, come on then.

He stands and walks to the broken window. Matchstick follows. Then me. Following Blaze. Back into the warehouse.

We're halfway when his phone rings. He says, *Yo. She's there? Now? Okay, tell her. Give it to her.* Then he hangs up.

Who was that? I ask.

Nobody, he says.

With the legal production of amphetamines topping ten billion tablets a year...the FDA and a panel of the National Academy of Sciences, known as the 'Task Force on Drug Abuse', recommended to a Senate subcommittee in 1971 that the potential for Ritalin abuse was such that it should be placed 'in the same strictly controlled classification as morphine and other valuable but dangerous drugs'.

Matthew Smith, *Hyperactive: The Controversial History of ADHD*

THE JOURNALIST

I've never been invited to morning conference before. Not even close. But today, without uttering a word, the editor's secretary taps me on the shoulder and beckons me to follow her. The meeting's already started by the time I go in, and I'm greeted with not much more than a couple of nods. Nobody speaks to me, and for almost half an hour I just sit there, listening while they plan the shape of tomorrow's paper. I take notes, not because there's anything I really need to write down, simply because it makes me feel less out of place. Then the editor turns to me, and without any kind of greeting asks if I've got a follow-up.

I tell him I have a lead I'd like to pursue.

"Okay," he says. "How long do you need?"

"Day or two."

"Fine."

That's it. Everyone stares but I just look at the pad on my lap and focus every brain cell on thinking, *Don't let them see how much you're enjoying this. Don't even smile. This isn't a treat, it isn't a gift, it isn't a favor, it's just what you've deserved all along, and if the others can't see it, that's their problem. If you act like you don't belong, you won't, so don't smile, don't be grateful, don't even look pleased.*

I walk out of the meeting with Alan, who runs my section. Before he can say anything, before he can give me any other work to do, I tell him I'm heading out on that story. He can call if he needs me.

Two minutes later I'm outside, standing in the hot, fetid embrace of London's August air. All around me I can see nothing but concrete, steel, and glass, but there's a muddy, fishy waft of river that smells like the leakage of an embarrassing truth. My skin immediately prickles as the pores open, ready to seep sweat.

Across the wide concourse between the tower blocks, workers are scurrying in purposeful diagonals, heads down, barreling on through their working day, same as yesterday, same as tomorrow. Watching them, I feel a momentary sensation of serene distance, as if for all their hurry, they are standing still, while despite my stillness, I am somehow in motion. This assignment is my chance. Everything I've ever worked for has led me toward this job, this piece, this moment. I have to get it right. The key to the door to the next level is in my hand. I mustn't fumble or hesitate.

I turn and head for the Tube. I need to go home and change.

The names of the hostage-takers aren't confirmed, but a few clues as to where they're from have just leaked out. Nobody has announced anything, but there's a Twitter buzz pointing toward the Aylesbury Estate in Southwark. I have a hunch that if I just go there somebody will tell me something, but I can't do it dressed for Canary Wharf. That would be like going to a soccer match in a ball gown. The journey is barely any distance, just a short hop across southeast London, but in other ways it's almost as far as you can travel.

Before stepping out of my apartment I check myself in the mirror. Superdry hoodie, Nike sneakers, Diesel jeans: my attempt at housing projects style. Scruffy/flashy/sporty/designer—the cheap-but-expensive look. I know the jeans are too middle-class, but I don't have a better option, and going the whole hog to leggings or jogging pants would be pushing it too far. I might look like I was mocking them. There has to be some kind of match between my clothes and my accent.

I leave my purse and jewelry at home. The only things I take are my house keys, my phone, and a few bills folded up small, shoved to the bottom of a pocket.

It feels strange to go anywhere without a bag. Every few seconds my brain seems to have a momentary panic—*MY BAG!!*—before I remind myself what I'm doing. A lot of men go through life like this, completely bagless, pockets jangling with stuff. It makes you walk differently, all this ballast swaying and clanking at the groin. Maybe they think it draws attention to their equipment. I can't think of any other reason for it, because this is definitely not a comfortable way to travel.

I take a cab to the projects but get the driver to pull up around the corner. I want to arrive on foot, unobtrusive. I don't want anyone to spot me as an outsider until I've had a chance to scope out the place.

The map on my phone tells me almost nothing. There's just a big empty gap alongside Thurlow Street, not even marked with any name, and that's the spot. A few roads thread into it, but there's no obvious entrance or exit. I'm assuming you can walk through, but it looks like a driver would have to go around the outside and slip in through the correct inlet. In this way it seems designed almost like a fortress, though whether that would be to keep people out or keep people in, I'm not so sure. Either way, it makes the place more or less invisible to anyone who isn't actually going in. The rest of us can just drive around the perimeter without even knowing that it exists, or that ten thousand people live there.

As the cabbie writes out my receipt, he asks if I'm visiting someone.

"Kind of," I say.

He gives me a skeptical look as he hands it over. "Watch out for yourself," he says, before winding up the window and driving off. It's not an exchange that fills me with confidence.

Should I be afraid? All the thousands of people who live there must go in and out all the time. I've seen a statistic saying there's a crime every four hours here, but there's no particular reason why anything would happen to me. However much crime there is, presumably most people get through most days without anything bad happening to them. Or anything actually criminal, anyway. The odds are in my favor. Besides, this is my only lead. If it was easy or obvious, there'd be hundreds of other journalists here ahead of me, and from where I'm standing it doesn't look like there's a single one.

Fear attracts aggression. I allow myself a few more seconds of anxiety, then decide to switch it off and walk in. Not too casual, not too curious, no photos, no notes.

I'm just going to walk through the place at a speed that makes me look like I know where I'm going and have a reason to be there.

The outer edge of housing, along the main road, is in the classic south London housing projects style. Garages and the odd shop at ground level, nine stories above in alternating stripes of concrete balconies and windows. Fans of iron spikes interrupt the long balconies at regular intervals, like bar lines on a stave.

A narrow road leads through a gap between two of these huge edifices, leading into that blank spot on the map. I walk in, treading gingerly over the cracked and pitted tarmac. On one side of the road is some kind of incinerator, a windowless concrete cube with one tall chimney pointing skyward. On the other is a fenced-in playground scattered with soccer-playing kids and teenagers. This is probably who I ought to talk to, but I decide to take a look around first.

At street level there are just garages. Above these are walkways, one of which snakes above my head, over the road, but it's not obvious how you'd get up to one of these walkways and into an actual apartment.

Inside the projects, there's more variation in the buildings. They are mostly lower rise, some concrete, some in what looks like eighties red brick. There are knee-high concrete posts everywhere, as if drivers in this place can't be trusted to stay on the roads, which perhaps they can't, because every road either loops back on itself or stops without warning, only to continue beyond a narrow strip of pavement protected by those gray, cracked posts. Great care has been taken to ensure this place can be driven into, but not through.

Apart from that playground, there's no open space. Just parking and more parking. Outside some of the more recent-looking buildings there are scraps of grass behind metal railings, either a useless private garden or a useless communal space, it's impossible to tell.

It is midmorning and there's hardly anyone around. The first person who walks past me is a middle-aged Indian woman in a sari. I try to stop her and ask if she knows anything about the hostage situation, but she doesn't even break stride or look at me. She just gives a faint headshake which seems to mean, *I have no interest in anything you could possibly say to me.* She may well have a point.

I try a pair of teenage girls next. They pause for a moment, stare at me with an odd mixture of blankness and hostility, then use two words to recommend that I leave.

I decide to head back toward the playground. It's not really a playground, just a fenced-in patch of tarmac, but at least the kids there aren't on the way to anywhere else. If I pick my moment, it will be harder for them to walk away.

I hover at the gate for a while, but I know I can't leave it too long. I don't want them to think I'm some kind of weirdo. So when the ball comes my way I trap it underfoot and, with an attempt at a relaxed smile, address the kid who comes to fetch it. He's white, thirteen-ish, skinny, and pale.

"Excuse me," I say. "I don't mean to bother you, but I'm a journalist and I've heard a rumor about these projects. Is there any chance you and your mates would talk to me for a minute or two?"

He grabs the ball and looks up at me. I'm a foot or so taller than him. His face is flushed and sweaty. He snorts, and for a moment I think he might be about to spit in my face.

He chucks the ball to one of his friends and spits on the ground behind him.

"What about?" he says.

"It's not about the riots," I say. "That's not my story."

"What about the riots?" he says.

"No, not that. It's about the hostage thing. You heard about that?"

"Maybe."

"What's she want?" It's another kid, taller, black, who pops up behind him. Moments later there's about seven of them, all around me.

Stupidly, I've stepped away from the gate, so I now have no exit route. The fence is at my back and there's a semicircle of boys in front of me.

Fear attracts aggression, I remind myself.

"I...I'm a journalist. I'm supposed to be researching the hostage situation. In Hackney. I've seen a rumor on Twitter that there's a connection to these projects. That some of the people involved are from here."

There's a sudden burst of laughter. One of the kids actually falls over. I hear a few of them repeat to one another in upper-class voices, "A rumor on Twitter...ooh, a rumor on Twitter...Is it a rumor? Is it on Twitter?..."

I find myself half smiling, more in relief that the hostility seems to have evaporated than through any understanding of what the joke actually is.

Eventually, the tallest of the kids addresses me. "You don't know who it is?"

"No."

"And you're a journalist?"

"The police haven't released the information."

"*Everyone* knows who it is, man. Fuck sake. What's wrong with you?"

"You know who it is?"

"Duh!"

"Who is it?"

"How much?"

"What?"

"How much? What's it worth?"

"I…er…"

"Twenty quid!"

"Twenty quid?"

"Yeah. Minimum."

"Er…okay." I reach into my pocket and separate out a single note from the tightly folded bundle. I tease it out carefully, making sure it doesn't pull any more money with it, and hand over the twenty pounds.

"Blaze," he says. "Blaze and his crew."

"Blaze?"

"Yeah, Blaze."

"Blaze? That's a name?"

The kid nods.

"Do you have a real name?"

The kid shrugs.

"How old is he?"

The kid shrugs.

"Roughly. Twelve? Fifteen? Twenty? Thirty?"

More laughter. "What are you talking about? He's a teenager. Like, fifteen, sixteen, something like that. *Thirty!* Shit, man!"

"And he lives in the projects?"

"Yeah."

"So his family's here?"

"Yeah."

"Do they know he's involved?"

The kid shrugs.

"Do you know where they live?"

He turns to another boy, with a dark, round Somali face. "Where'd's Blaze live?"

The black kid examines me for a moment, as if he's calculating something in his head. "How much?" he says.

All the boys laugh again. One of them, slapping a friend on the arm, says, "Yeah, man. How much. You tell her."

"Ten quid?" I say.

"Twenty."

"You have to take me. Not just tell me."

"Deal," he says.

"I'll pay you when we're there."

"You don't trust me?"

"You don't trust him?"

"Why don't you trust him?"

"How do I know you won't just run off?"

"She don't trust me!"

"I don't trust you!" says his friend.

More laughter. Without any real menace, the round-faced boy kicks the other kid on the thigh, then turns and walks out of the playground.

"Come on, then," he says to me.

He walks off, and I follow. He doesn't even glance back at me as he leads on through the projects. We cross a small area of broken paving stones dotted with overflowing Dumpsters, past the incinerator, down a narrow road, beside a long line of garages topped by three or four stories of narrow-windowed concrete buildings, the balconies festooned with laundry, children's bikes, satellite dishes, and semi-cast-off furniture. Some of the balconies are enclosed by metal bars. From the way the place is constructed, you'd think it was a settlement for thousands of cars, with human accommodation added on up high and out of the way, like the staff quarters in a hotel.

There don't seem to be any other pedestrians, or shops, or billboards, which gives the place a dead feel that seems to match the idea of it being represented by an empty space on the map. It feels both fully inhabited and semi-abandoned, not like part of London at all. There isn't even much graffiti, which I can't imagine has much to do with civic pride. Perhaps this place doesn't even seem worth defacing. The garage doors, unlike most garage doors in the city, are mostly untagged, though they are all scrawled with "DO NOT PARK HERE" in drippy paint.

One garage has a layer of mottled, slatted glass above it, bearing a message in yellow stick-on capital letters: "WENDOVER T&RA MEETING ROOM." If the boy were next to me I might ask him what that means, but he's still up ahead, maintaining a loping pace that somehow makes it clear he doesn't want me to catch up and walk with him. He doesn't turn around, but he must be listening, because when I speed up, he speeds up, keeping the same few meters between us.

When he comes to a high edifice of concrete, bearing a sign in a bulky sixties typeface saying "MISSENDEN 166–255," he makes a sharp turn, leading me down a wider street between two rows of low-rise redbrick housing to which somebody seems to have tacked on plumbing as an afterthought. Pipes snake down the outside of the building spewing deltas of white scurf as if the entire building stopped weeping a while ago but never wiped away the tears.

Around the next corner, a nine-story concrete block appears in front of us, as long as a soccer pitch. Our road curves to the right and goes underneath it, through a cavity painted lurid purple. The boy goes ahead, through the tunnel, without turning back.

I pause for a moment and look around. There is nobody else on the street. Despite all the garages and all the parked cars, not one vehicle is moving. It occurs to me for the first time that this could be a trick. As far as I can see, I'm now alone. I can't see into this tunnel, or through to the other side.

In fact, I'm only assuming there is another side. This could just be a hollow under the building for garbage or access, a hidden spot perfect for mugging. Or worse.

Like one of those optical illusions that suddenly pops in your visual cortex, turning a young man into an old woman, I realize what I am doing, where I am, who I'm following. What appeared logical flips into foolhardy stupidity.

I still have a choice. I can just turn and walk away, but if this kid means me any harm, he and his friends will find me and do whatever it is they want to do. I'm not even sure I know how to retrace my steps out of the projects. And if I just take off in a different direction, there's no knowing where I'll find myself.

The boy doesn't reappear from the tunnel. He's either waiting for me in there, or he's carried on. I sense that he knows I've stopped, and he must suspect what I'm thinking.

It's the memory of morning conference that pushes me on again. I've got that key in my hand. If I don't push myself forward, find the lock, open the door, I may never get another chance. Journalism is a dying profession. If I want to keep my place I have to move on and up. Anyone who stands still is next in line for the sack.

"Fear attracts aggression," I mutter to myself. "Fear attracts aggression."

A few steps, and I can see through the tunnel. It's the height and length of an articulated truck. I can see light on the other side, and the boy is there, waiting for me. He isn't moving, and his face is expressionless, cast downward, neither looking at me nor not looking at me.

There's something sinister, catlike, in this stillness, this patience. I can still run away.

But I walk on, through the urine-smelling purple hollow. As soon as he sees that I'm coming, the boy turns away and keeps on walking. A pulse of relief radiates through my chest. If he wanted to jump me, this was the spot for it.

I emerge in an oval cul-de-sac surrounded by more garages, topped by a concrete walkway along a building of four layers: doors, balconies, wall, windows. In the middle, a row of sickly trees is growing out of a patch of scrubby, densely packed soil.

Above me, I see something that makes my spirits plummet. Halfway down the nearest balcony, outside one of the doors, is a crowd, sipping coffee from take-out cups, chatting, fiddling with laptops and cameras. Journalists.

When I turn, the boy is next to me, with his hand out and a smirk on his face.

"Twenny," he says.

"You never told me there were other journalists here!"

"You never aksed."

"It's *asked*, not *aksed*," I snap.

He shrugs. "Twenny."

I hand him the money and he walks away. There barely seems any point in continuing, but since I'm there, I decide to press on.

The men outside the door nudge one another and quietly laugh at me as I approach. I'm not sure how, but it's obvious that I'm broadsheet and they're tabloid. I should have known these guys would be here before me. They specialize in this kind of stuff. They can find anyone, anywhere.

They give me a sarcastic round of slow applause, hailing me with mocking congratulations at the speed with which I've found the place. I don't respond.

There was nothing on any news sites when I set off, but it's probably up there for anyone to see now. I was dreaming if I thought I could be the first. The only thing I can do now is put a note through the door, but I'm bagless. I don't have pen or paper. All I can find is my taxi receipt.

The whole crowd of guys is watching me and they know exactly what I'm thinking.

"Ain't you got a pen?" says one of them.

"She don't even have a pen!"

More laughter, some genuine, some rasping and forced out for the pleasure of putting me in my place.

One of the photographers passes me a ballpoint, to the sound of groans and a wolf whistle.

I scribble out the taxi driver's writing and on the back scrawl down my name, newspaper, phone number, and the words CALL ME. As I shove the scrap of paper through the tiny, stiff letterbox, there's another little ripple of laughter.

"What you offering? Two pound fifty in Argos vouchers?"

"A bag of chips?"

"Ticket to the ballet?"

I don't know what these papers will have offered, but it'll be thousands, tens of thousands, just for any kind of interview. I feel so ridiculous, I can't make eye contact with a single one of them. Rushing away would seem like an acknowledgment of my humiliation, so I slip to the edge of the crowd and take out my phone, typing into it as if I'm engrossed in sending an important message.

A voice calls out asking if I'm trying to get another Argos voucher out of my editor, but I pretend not to hear.

Then, after a few minutes, something extraordinary happens. The door opens—just a crack—held firm by a fastened security chain. There's a moment of panicked silence, followed by frantic activity as shutters click and whirr. A black face—sort of young, sort of middle-aged—is visible in the dimly lit space between the wood-veneer door and its chipped, metal-reinforced frame. A cacophony of questions is hurled at her. She flinches under the onslaught, and when she eventually speaks, she seems to say just a couple of words, both of them entirely inaudible.

The crowd hushes. A barrage of microphones and Dictaphones almost obscures her from view. She speaks again.

"Who's Amanda?" she says.

For a moment, I'm too shocked to respond. After a puzzled silence, I say, "It's me," and step forward.

A hand comes out through the gap and passes me a scrap of paper. The instant it is in my grasp, the door closes.

On the paper is a number, scrawled in blue ink. Five plumply inscribed digits, then below that six more. A cell phone number. I close my fist, concealing it from view, and look up. Every person there is staring at me, jaw open.

"What is it?" says one of them.

"Good luck, fellas," I reply, with a mock-sympathetic smile, before turning on my heel and walking away. Except that I'm not really walking, it's more like floating, because at this moment gravity just can't touch me.

One mother was told that her son did not really need Ritalin, but her physicians suggested to her that 'to please the school, why don't you give him them anyway?'

Matthew Smith, *Hyperactive: The Controversial History of ADHD*

LEE

I swear, weirdest thing of all is, it's boring

yeah, it's the maddest thing we ever done by miles, but it's on and on now day after day

no TV, no Xbox, I swear I'm bored

explored everywhere, nothing left to find, nothing left to smash, just some old bloke tied to a radiator needing to be taken for pisses all the time

and Blaze makes me go on lookout up at the top window and I don't even know what for, 'cause there's nothing to see

Femi don't turn up for his shift this afternoon, so I just give up and go down and he ain't there, but then he comes in with Blaze and Matchstick from out back with a weird look on his face like someone's died

nobody says nothing, so I don't go back and Femi don't either, so maybe Blaze has realized the lookout's pointless

and after that nothing happens, literally nothing, so I go up to the big room that's got nothing left in it except that massive wooden table that you can't get out the door, but I'm thinking it must have got in

so I go for it, using it like a battering ram until one of the doors comes off the hinges, then I've got it out on the balcony and I just keep pushing and pushing right up to the railings, and I push some more—up up up—and I shout a warning, then over it goes

BOOOOM!

and I look down and it ain't even smashed, it's just at a weird angle, kind of sad, with two broken legs at one end and a crack down the middle

and the others is looking up at me not saying nothing, just the same look on all their faces like, *What was the point of that?*

so I laugh, but it don't sound right; it's kind of embarrassed

then I go down and nothing else happens and then it's dark and there's no drinking, no music, no messing about, nothing; we all just get out the boxes that's like our beds and lie down

boring

This sudden emergence of a genetic disorder is puzzling...
Naughty and disruptive children have doubtless always
existed. In the past their unruly behaviour might have been
ascribed to poor parenting, poverty, impoverished schools, or
unsympathetic teachers...Now we blame the victim instead;
there is original sin in them there genes.

Steven Rose, 'Neurogenetic determinism and the new
euphenics', *BMJ*

BLAZE

Don't sleep. Never sleep. Specially not on that sofa, man, no
room, not enough space, Karen all stretched out hogging it
all. Wouldn't be no different without her, though, I just ain't
a sleeper, never have been. Too much to think about, too
many voices, talk talk talk, too much to figure out. Not crazy
voices, not schizo shit, just my own head chatting away,
won't ever shut up. No off switch. Don't know how everyone else does it, wish I did.

Can't just lie there all night not sleeping, drives you mental.

I get up, stretch, scratch, do that thing with my neck that
makes it click and eases some of the stiffness. It's hot in
here, man, day and night, always hot.

Look down at Karen, naked on that shitty sofa, one arm
hanging down toward the floor. She got an awesome body,
just the swooping shape of it, I swear it's proof there's a
God right there, 'cause you can't imagine nothing better,
nothing you'd rather see. So peaceful, just lying there right in
front of me, but in her head she's miles away, somewhere so
quiet and calm I can't never get there. I go in proper close to

see what it looks like. Tiny pool of sweat in the V at the bottom of her neck, going up and down with each breath. I want to lick it up but ain't fair to wake her, so I don't. Her eyes is flicking left right left, you can see the bulge under the eyelid where they move, she's away somewhere chasing something, all busy, doing I don't know what, and probably she'll never know, neither. Whole eyeball seems to go in deeper, sink into her head when she's asleep. Robs her of something, it's almost a dead look to her face. Ain't the same her, without all that front, without the chat and the attitude, it's like she's almost hollow, you know?

She's fine, she's as fine a woman as I'm ever going to get, but I don't know, there's something not there and you can see it when she's asleep, see what's missing. The way she looks, all fox, it's a mask, ain't it? Blinds you to what's underneath, and with Karen I sometimes think there ain't nothing underneath. Not literally nothing, but nothing for nobody else. Nothing real, nothing proper real, so when you look at her you're actually seeing her and she's actually seeing you, like a real connection, that's what you don't get. Ain't complaining, just telling it how it is.

I lean closer, put an ear on her, all gentle so she don't wake. It's so late, so quiet, I can hear it perfect, the *badum badum badum,* on and on, all day and all night, just inside under the skin. Amazing, when you think about it. We all got one, goes on and on, never getting tired, never fussing about whatever crazy shit is going on all around, just *badum badum badum* till one day it stops and you're dead.

Only seen a dead man once, it was a stabbing at a party. Can't never forget it. When you seen that you don't never forget. I tell you, dead eyes got a look that cuts into you like a shank, it's like staring into the coldest, darkest, farthest thing you ever seen and you know it's the worst place and we're all going there, we all got our time coming. Never felt mine was far away, neither. Always felt like it was just around the next corner, always, now more than ever. I ain't afraid of much, ain't afraid of no man, but I'm afraid of that.

Ain't good, thoughts going dark this time of night. This is the dead hour when all the worst things come back, memories I can't let in, bitter fantasies, revenge that ain't never going to happen on the people that messed with me, just bullshit chasing itself around and around my head till I'm dizzy and more awake than ever.

I pull on my Calvins, walk out. Got to move somewhere, do something, keep my head straight.

Down the stairs, creaky rusted metal with a row of little holes in each step to stop you slipping, harsh on bare feet, then concrete at the bottom, flat, cool and proper nice. Need to watch out for nails and glass, but it's worth it to feel that cold concrete on the skin.

Lee's got the armchair for once. Always after a go in the armchair, makes him feel important, but nobody wants it at night, so he gets it. His mouth's open like always, chin lolling to the side. Femi's on a pile of flattened-out boxes over by the door, across it so nobody can come in without waking him. Troy's doing the same at the doorway where the hostage is.

I go over and it's weird watching Troy sleep. Ain't never seen it before. He looks even smaller than normal, even more like something that might just break at any moment. Only time I ever seen him relaxed, not alert, not looking around for where the danger's heading in from. He's wired up tight, Troy, so tight on a frame that don't seem strong enough for it. Don't know when, but someday it'll all snap—just collapse—can't live a whole life the way he does, it ain't possible.

I step around him and go in to the hostage. Troy loosens him at night, gives him some cardboard for a pillow, but he don't really look asleep. Something in his eyes. They're shut but they ain't flicking like Karen's, aren't sunk in or far away, and his breathing ain't sleep breathing, I can just tell, even though his eyes are closed and he ain't moving.

I go up and poke him with my toe. He don't move, but his eyelids flash open, terror right there, straightaway. Feels good to stand over him, naked except my Calvins, and he got to look up at me towering over him, 'cause I'm buff, I'm ripped, it's just a fact, and he's this lardy little white guy and I don't need to say nothing, just look at him, stare at him, and he knows what's what. Don't need to speak, less I say the better. Just wake him, stare, freak him out. It's beautiful.

He's mine. Ain't never known nothing like it in my whole life. He's mine.

Sometimes just yesterday or the day before disappears like it was never even there, but the day we took the guy, that's so strong in my head I can walk up to it and touch it, feel it, glossy and crisp like the front of a magazine. It was a beautiful day, perfect, the sky all bluest blue, criss-crossed with plane tracks. Days like that I always look up for the plane tracks, follow them across the sky, wondering where they're going, wishing it was me.

One day I want to go in a plane. Just once. It ain't never going to happen, but that's what I want, just once in my life to be up there in the blue and I wouldn't even look down—I don't care about that—I'd look out and up and around and just knowing that I was flying, that would be enough. People act like it's normal, like flying is normal, but it ain't. Just once before I die I want to know what it's like.

So it was a day like that, a good sky day in the sky and also in my head, just everything popping good and sharp. And when the riot kicked off we all went for a look and I didn't even feel like I was in it, like I was really there, I just thought we're floating through this, we're here and we're not here, and it was so beautiful, the fires and the people all working together smashing up the shops, and the police cowering under their shields, just great, and the floating was so fine, but also like I was in a bubble. Thing is, I didn't want to float, didn't want to miss it, I wanted to be in it, inside it, feeling it, 'cause it might never happen again, then I thought it's stupid just smashing stuff up and stealing crap, and it came to me like a lump of gold landing in the palm of my hand, I just knew that I had to do something real, something extreme, something that wasn't copying everyone else, but was an actual idea from my own head.

An idea ain't one thing. It's two. Two quiet, slow, sleepy things in different places, woken up by a flash of electricity that jumps from one to the other, bringing them to life. That's the idea—the zing of the connection. There was the riot, the anger, the burning stuff, the revenge, the release of knowing that even though you're trapped and you've got no hope and no chance you're in a place where for once you're fighting back—that was thing one. Thing two was a place. Me and Matchstick found it a few weeks before. Just exploring. Crossing railway tracks to look for weirdness, forgotten spots, abandoned factories, it's something we do, I don't know why. Like a dare, but not really. Just checking stuff out for no reason.

You can figure the rest. Lightning flashed from one to the other, and that's why I'm here, now, staring at a guy tied to a radiator. That's why it happened. Or maybe it's a how rather than a why, but who knows if there's really a difference anyway? Stuff that happens happens 'cause there's an opportunity for it to happen. Who says anyone's actually choosing for it to happen or making it happen?

Yeah, looks like I chose it, like I caused it, but that ain't how it felt at the time. Didn't feel like I was having the idea, felt like the idea was having me. It was electric, man, powerful like you wouldn't believe. You know those guys on TV, on the screens in betting shops, riding horses full gallop, I mean, are they really in charge? Are they really telling the horse where to go? Don't look like it. That's what it felt like for me with this idea, and if you don't know what that feels like, if you never been lifted up and carried off by a buzzy plan for something bad you just got to do, then I feel sorry for you.

I knew the others would come with me. They can't resist. When I'm on fire, when it's all going on, nobody can resist, I'm king. It's just a fact, people follow me, I don't even got to ask them, they just do. Half the time I wish they didn't, half the time I think it's a curse, but there's nothing I can do about it, that's just how things are. I ain't being arrogant, it's just the truth.

Them days, them clear days when everything makes sense and your brain just speaks in one voice, and it's a calm voice taking you from step to step like a song where every note just has to be the one that it is, after the last one and before the one that comes next, them days are special and they don't last. There's always an afterward, when everything looks different, and the confusion comes back and what seemed obvious and true and right suddenly makes no sense.

That's how it was waking up on the sofa, next morning, slices of sunlight coming in through the blinds, striping over me and Karen, stripes that were straight and not straight, wobbling over the curves of our bodies. It was a good night, a sleep night, but waking up then I knew this whole thing wasn't so clever, and it all got done proper fast but that didn't mean it could be undone, not fast, not slow, not no way at all. Straight off, with a new day ahead, I saw there wasn't no way out, no way forward or back or nothing. We did good to get this far, but even if we set the guy free and ran off, they'd get us. I just woke up knowing we were done in, all of us. We'd jumped into a deep hole and there wasn't no ladder.

I don't know how many years you get for something like this, but I know the time we got here in this warehouse, with the hostage, the time we got between now and the first set of handcuffs, that's the only freedom we got for a long time. Pretty soon, I ain't never going to breathe free like this, not for years. I better drink it in while I can.

The guy's shut his eyes again. He can't look at me. Don't blame him.

I walk away, don't even know where, just walking.

My beautiful idea, my galloping horse, now it don't look so slick, but it brought us here, so all I can do is try and decide what next. Ain't no point giving up, 'cause screwed is screwed. Whatever they got in mind for our punishment, as long as we don't hurt the guy, there's nothing we can do now to make it worse or better. What's coming is coming, so we might as well enjoy the time we got left. But that don't mean I got a plan. That don't mean I got a clue.

I had some beautiful hours with Karen on that sofa. There's something about the warehouse, about being locked in with this guy, makes the whole thing feel like a vacation.

Never had one, but I seen the pictures, adverts of it every-where, smiling people just relaxing on the sand, no work, no worries, nothing. That's why it's like a vacation, 'cause it feels like time's stopped—like day and night has drifted together. Even with the feds right outside. That just makes it stronger, knowing we're surrounded, and we're living in a bubble that ain't got long before it bursts. It's sort of like feeling brand-new, made fresh, and also right about to die, all at once. Sometimes, boxed in here, nothing happening, I feel like I can actually hold a second, each second, as a thing in the palm of my hand, a little smooth pebble of time. Just catch one, and feel it, and drop it, then catch the next one.

But now Troy's showed me the news on his phone, the Concentr8 story, everything's flipped into a new place. Took me a while to digest it, had to hide away and think, didn't even want Karen or nobody, then I just burned the stuff and everyone except Troy looked at me like I'd lost my shit.

Maybe they still think I've gone mental, 'cause nobody's asked why. Femi had his little flip-out, but he still didn't ask why I burned the stuff. Troy doesn't need to ask, but them others, they're too scared, too dumb. Sheep.

Sometimes I see that look, that way people look at me, almost cringing with fear like I've made a part of them shrivel up, and it's a surprise, 'cause I don't even know what's going on or what they're afraid of. I know I get angry, but I don't hurt nobody, hardly ever. Weirdest thing of all is that sometimes it scares me when people do it, 'cause it makes me wonder if there's something going to come along and grab me and make me do bad shit I don't even want to do.

That time I got expelled, for what I did to the Turkish kid in the playground, honestly, I hardly even knew what was happening. He was asking for it, and he basically made me do it, and I just wasn't powerful enough to hold back the surge that took me over. Blaming me is like blaming the sky for raining. If I weren't carrying the shank it wouldn't have been nothing serious, but I ain't safe without it, and that ain't my fault.

After I burned them pills there was a weird atmosphere, everyone quiet, kind of suspicious, just not such a laugh no more. Different vibe took over, flat and cold and almost boring. There's message after message on my phone from Mum—on and on about what am I doing, where's Matchstick, where am I, then after that tons of chat about all the journalists outside, hassling her, trapping her in the apartment, on and on. I ain't really told her what I done—just too much grief trying to speak to her—but after I saw the Concentr8 story I told her there's one journalist I will talk to. Just one. Told her it might get them off her back, but don't even know if she heard, 'cause she's too busy telling me to turn myself in, but that's Mum, ain't it? Always fretting.

Then today after I got Femi off the roof she called and said the person was there. The journalist. I swear she's pushy, 'cause that lady been calling and calling all afternoon, leaving a message every time. I ain't answered, not yet, I ain't an idiot, but I listened to the messages, listened again and again, till I got that posh voice buzzing in my brain, stuck there.

Didn't know what to do about it—all afternoon thought maybe the whole thing was a stupid mistake—but you can think clearer in the dark—when you know you're on your own and ain't nobody going to interrupt you or hassle you—and suddenly I get that sparky tingle in my head and it's almost like I'm riding something again, like something's carrying me out of this weird misty place to somewhere else where the air's clear and good, 'cause out of nowhere I get this feeling of a direction ahead of me—an idea of what I can do.

Can't even wait till morning, neither—'cause everything always looks different in the mornings and I don't want to lose the feeling—don't want to change my mind. It's the middle of the night, but she ain't going to complain, is she?

Take out my phone. Dial.

"You called me."

"Who is this?" Her voice is sleepy. Confused.

"You called me. My mum gave you the number."

"It's you! God! Er...hi...great. Thanks for calling back. That's great! I...er...what time is it? Have you got a minute to talk?"

"You want to meet?"

"Meet? I thought you were—"

"There's a way out. Can't tell you how, but I can get out for about an hour, I reckon. You know the KFC in Hackney?"

"Er...not off hand, but I can find it."

"Few doors up from the Empire."

"I'll find it."

"You'll come alone?"

"Of course."

"You ain't gonna fuck me over."

"I just want to talk to you."

"If you ain't alone, you won't find me."

"I'll be alone."

"Tomorrow. Ten."

Hang up. Don't know why, but I'm smiling. For all I know she ain't who she says she is. For all I know she's a fed and they're going to jump me soon as I show up. But at least I done something, at least I got a plan, got something to do. It ain't a way out, but it's a way forward, and that feels sweet, feels better than the flatness that's squashed us down all day, and I don't even notice climbing the stairs or choosing to go there, but now Karen's in front of me, peaceful like a sheet of fresh snow, naked and perfect, and I kiss her, not much more than just brushing against her lips, and at first she's asleep but then she ain't and she puts her hands on my cheeks and looks at me and I swear that for once she really is looking at me, looking right into me, then she pulls my face toward hers and we're kissing again and my Calvins are off, and I got my hands all over her, all at once, don't know how, that's just what it feels like, and she's all around me like water, wrapping me into her, and I'm lifting her but she don't weigh nothing, and I'm pushing her into the wall, pushing into her, and I swear it's like we're one person and I can't hear nothing but I can also hear everything, and feel everything, and it's like there ain't nothing in the universe except the feeling of this, building and building till it's almost too much to take, too much to believe, too much for a body to hold without exploding.

Those lines of sun, straight but not straight, are on us when we wake, don't know how much later, tangled up together on the floor. There's a pigeon gargling on the windowsill outside, the London dawn chorus. I ain't scared, I'm feeling proper good, but I got a feeling it might be the last one I ever hear.

Day Five

I can't tell you how many teachers and school nurses have told me how concerned they've become at the volume of kids they see every day at their schools who are on ADHD medication... and with 13.2% of boys being diagnosed compared to 5.6% of girls, I started to wonder if boys were being medicated for simply being boys, and if their "disorder" was really just a very normal phase of development.

Bronwen Hruska interviewed by Jasmine Elist, *LA Times*

THE JOURNALIST

Questions jitter through my head as I ride the Tube, then the bus, toward Hackney. How do I approach him? What am I looking for? A motive? The story of his life? An insider account of the riots? A voice of the people or the voice of the devil? Blaze is this week's public enemy number one, so should I look for evidence to back up the story everyone wants to hear, or use my access to find a more surprising angle—a way to pitch the guy as something more than just a feral punk? Maybe planning what I want to write before the interview is the wrong approach. Perhaps I just need to be alert, be receptive, and trust my instincts. Talk to him. Draw him out. Dig for as much material as I can get, then worry about the angle later.

But if I don't know what I'm looking for, how do I know which questions to ask? I need to approach this professionally, with a plan. This is my moment, my scoop. I have to do my job, think on my feet, and get it right.

The bus sets me down outside the Hackney Empire on Mare Street. There were major flare-ups here earlier in the week, but the last couple of nights things seem to have calmed down. Nobody quite knows why. The police are saying that saturating the streets with officers from around the country has done the trick, but this claim feels like a stretch. Almost as if the whole thing was a natural event, a storm that simply comes, then goes in its own time, the chaos seems to have subsided, moved away without explanation or warning, just as it arrived.

Most of Mare Street is still shuttered up. The carcass of a burned-out double decker bus, skewed as if in the middle of a U-turn, blocks two lanes. An ashy burned-plastic smell is still hanging in the air. A few shopkeepers seem to have drifted back to the battlefield, and can be seen sweeping up broken glass or examining the wreckage of their shops. Some outlets have been picked clean, others left untouched. A solicitor's office has been comprehensively torched; a pawnshop trashed beyond repair. Vengeance, perhaps, alongside the theft.

People used to make burned offerings to appease the gods. Something in the nightly performance of these conflicts, set up at specific locations with an evening commencement and a daytime lull, reminds me of this. It feels like a ritual, an outbreak of seeming chaos choreographed to unspoken rules, drawing to a close when catharsis has been achieved. However real the anger, however real the damage, on some level the whole thing felt like a performance.

That's just my opinion, though, and no use whatsoever as journalism. What I need is a clutch of juicy quotes from this guy Blaze. Something inflammatory, something offensive, a gory anecdote from his childhood. That's journalism.

I step into KFC and scan the room for anyone who might be him. There are plenty of teenagers, plenty of black kids, but nobody alone, and nobody who looks up at me. If he were here, he would have spotted me immediately. White, middle class, I stand out in the Hackney KFC like a pig in a field of cows.

Blaze chose this place well. If I brought anyone with me, even if they arrived separately, it would be easy to spot.

I order myself a coffee and, as an afterthought, a bag of French fries, more because I want something to do with my hands than through any genuine desire to eat them. I also get the feeling it will make me look less out of place if I'm eating something, rather than perching tensely at an empty table clutching a drink.

There's an old saying that you shouldn't order food in any restaurant that has more items on the menu than there are chairs. Hackney KFC passes this test—it's a small menu—but falls down on another old maxim of dining lore, which says that any restaurant where the furniture is bolted to the floor probably isn't so great either.

I take a seat at the least greasy table, choosing one set back away from the window, and wait.

Why *do* they bolt the chairs down? Has anyone ever stolen a chair from a restaurant while it was actually open? And if you did want to steal a chair from a restaurant, is KFC the place you'd choose?

I bite into a "French fry." It crumbles into a paste that is both gooey and dusty, filling my mouth with wafts of over-powering tastelessness.

The instant he walks in, I know this is Blaze. He looks straight at me for one thing, but it's not just that. It's the way he carries himself. He's got that stride you see on athletes who can conceal their speed. It's a way the body moves when it's perfectly balanced, seeming to have more time than the rest of us, every movement sculpted from faultless curves and arcs.

He wordlessly reaches out a hand to shake mine, looking at me, right into me, with dark, heavy-lidded eyes that seem older than the rest of him. His hand wraps right around mine, and I can feel the strength in his fingers, even though he gives my palm only a gentle squeeze.

"How old are you?" he says as he sits.

"*What?*" This is the last thing I was expecting him to say. I haven't been greeted like this for more than twenty years.

"I just mean you ain't as old as I was expecting."

"You want something to eat?" I say, dodging the question.

"I'll have a bucket of wings."

"Drink?"

"Coke. You can meal it."

I have no idea what this means, but I repeat the formula at the counter and am given the wings, a vat of drink, and a cardboard container of fries, all for less money than a deli sandwich.

As he works his way through the first few chicken wings he doesn't speak, and I get the strange feeling that I shouldn't, either. Seeing him, feeling his presence, my instinct is that I should take things slow, not be too eager or overtly curious. Play it as a chat rather than an interview. I make a snap decision and decide to leave the Dictaphone in my bag. I can do this by memory. It's not as if he's going to sue me for misquoting him. I need to keep him relaxed and draw him out. For any quotes, the gist will do. It doesn't have to be word perfect.

"So how's things at the warehouse?" I say. Nothing too direct. Nothing too challenging.

"Pretty chilled."

"The hostage is okay?"

"First things first," he snaps. "You don't print nothing about my mum. Nothing."

"Er…okay, nothing about your mum."

"Don't go there again. Leave her alone."

"All right."

"You better."

"I will. I was asking you about the hostage."

"We're looking after him. He'll be fine."

"You're not going to hurt him?"

"Got no plans to," he says, sucking at a bone, a mischievous twinkle darting across his face. There's something unsettling about the speed with which he can flick from relaxed to threatening and back again. I already sense that if I say the wrong thing he might just stand up and walk out. He can't hurt me. Not here, not in public, with the entire Metropolitan Police Force looking for him, but I wouldn't want to be alone with the guy.

"Have you got any demands?" I say, fighting back the tension that is clenching my windpipe. I need to stay calm and get the important questions out of the way quickly. This interview could end any second.

He pushes away the wings and starts on his fries, lifting his chin and looking at me down his nose, assessing me. "I got a demand off of you," he says. He's leaning far back now, his legs spread wide, non-eating hand resting in his lap.

"Yes? What's that?" My pulse accelerates, a trickle of fear seeping into my veins. He's already taken one hostage, perhaps he wants another. Perhaps this whole meeting is some kind of setup.

"You wrote that stuff? About Concentr8? That was you?"

"Yes."

For the next quarter hour, the interview flips. He questions me, on and on, exploring every detail, testing my evidence, digging out everything I know about Concentr8, about what it is, how it's given out, who changed the policy on its distribution and how. He knows most of it already, has the whole article from the previous day's paper clear in his head, but he presses for more, squeezing me for every drop of information I have.

This kid is sharp. He looks slow, but he doesn't miss anything and no logical inconsistency gets past him. Born somewhere else, he could have become anything. With my education he could have ended up doing my job, no trouble. But it's pretty clear he's going to spend most of his life in jail.

His questions spiral back again and again to the heart of the story. "So they said they was helping us, but they was actually drugging us up to keep us quiet?"

"That's a question of interpretation," I say, "but it is beginning to look like that."

"Everybody wins, yeah? Schools, teachers, feds, parents? Everyone."

"Looks like it."

"Except the kids that are taking the pills."

"You tell me. What does it feel like to be on them?"

"Don't even know who I'd be if I'd never had it, do I? No idea what it's done to my head."

"It's been out of circulation for a while now. Everyone's saying that's one of the reasons for the riots. Isn't it?"

"Yeah."

"So do you feel different since it was taken away?"

"Yeah, but you get used to taking it, don't you? That's why people wanted it back. But that just makes it worse, don't it?"

"Why?"

"*Why?* Fuck sake, man! These same people locking people up over and over for drugs, for weed, talking about that stuff on and on like it's the devil's work, then they can't even see that getting us hooked on some other shit is the exact same thing. When we do it, it's a crime. When they do it, it's...I don't know...social work."

"You think it's the same thing as drug dealing?"

"'Course it is! Why are people out on the streets? They're hooked! It's the same story. Filling your body with shit that fucks your brain is bad enough, but when it's shit that makes you want it even when it's fucking you? Yeah, that's dealing. What else is it?"

"I don't know."

"What else is it?"

"I don't know."

"Tell me. What is it?" He isn't shouting, but there's steel in his voice.

My heart begins to race again, though not with fear. This time I think it's shame. Blaze can see that the connection had never occurred to me. I feel as if he's found something in me that I didn't even know was there, as if he's rooted out some core prejudice.

"What is it?" he repeats, still quiet, but icy with anger.

It's against all my journalistic principles to answer his question. This interview isn't about me or my opinions. It isn't important what I think, at least it ought not to be, but Blaze won't let the question go. He's silent, waiting for my answer, and I can see he won't move on until he has one.

All my plans, all the options I had in my head for how to write up this interview, now feel useless. Blaze has done something to me. The most unexpected sensation has taken me over. I feel as if I am on his side.

"Okay," I say. "I suppose it is the same thing."

"Yeah. Hurts you to say it, though, don't it?"

"It's just a surprising idea."

"To you, maybe. Listen, I got you here 'cause I wanted to hear this shit from the source. I wanted to get it straight in my head and know for sure what's what. But I got a plan I want you to help me with. You need a story, yeah? That's why you're here?"

"I suppose."

"I got you a story."

"You've given me one already."

"No, I got you a proper story."

"What's that?"

"You said do we got demands?"

"Do you?"

"Sort of. It ain't exactly a demand."

"What is it?"

"I won't talk to the feds—they're dicks—but I will talk to the mayor. One to one. Man to man."

He's right. That *is* a story.

"You can set that up?" he asks.

"I can't set it up, but I can publish the request. He'll have to respond."

"Cool."

"I'll do it on one condition," I say.

"You'll do it anyway."

"One condition."

"What's that?"

"If the meeting happens, I get to come."

He looks at me, sucking the stripy red straw that protrudes from his Coke. A smirk plays across his lips as he puts the drink down. "You can't get enough of me, can you?"

It's hard to be sure, but I suddenly feel as if Blaze might be flirting.

"You're the story," I say. My cheeks, for some reason, feel slightly hotter than they did a few seconds ago.

"That's your condition? Without that, you won't write nothing? You'll pretend you never came here, never met me?"

"Are you messing with me?"

"Yeah, I'm messing with you. But fuck it, you can come. Why not?" He takes another suck at his Coke, swivels his head, takes a quick scan of the room, and stands up. "You think he'll do it?" he asks, flicking up his hood.

"I have no idea."

I so need Ritalin. Who's got a prescription? Am I sounding like a junkie?

Twitter

KAREN

So I wake up and he ain't there? And I'm thinking, oh he must be down with the others or something, but he ain't— 'cause when I go down and ask they're all like, *I thought he was up there with you.*

So we look around and it ain't no thing at first, but gradually we're looking in more and more places and I swear he is gone. He ain't nowhere. And it's Femi who gets stressed about it first? Even before we looked around the whole place, he's already, *He's stitched us up, he's done a runner, I'm going to kill him.* I mean, at first nobody's listening, it's just Femi sounding off like he does—he wouldn't kill nobody, least of all Blaze—but even if we don't think he's right you can feel the suspicion soaking into the rest of us. Even Matchstick looks worried.

Troy ain't giving nothing away, but he's with us looking for him—which he wouldn't if he really knew where Blaze was and if he was coming back.

So it's all like bubbling on a bit tense but nothing too crazy until Femi turns on Matchstick? That's when I'm like, *Oh, shit.*

Grabs him by the arm and says, *Listen, ain't nobody looking after you, now you got to take us all out of here. Where you took me before—was that the actual way out or just something to mess with me?*

Matchstick looks up at him, his eyes going all big, and you can see he ain't going to say nothing. Femi can push it as far as he likes, Matchstick ain't going to speak.

Shakes him. I swear he's half his size so it looks weird the two of them squaring off for what would be the stupidest fight ever.

Tell me, you little prick!

Nothing.

You want me to take you up there? Just me and you? See what happens? Mess you up like you did with me. You think you could take it?

I ain't never seen Matchstick cry, but I swear he's close now. That's when Troy steps in.

Let go of him, he says.

Fuck off.

Let go, says Troy, proper steel, even though Femi's a head taller, could have him no trouble. Matchstick twists while Femi's distracted, swerves away, runs to the corner under the pile of tires. Now it's Femi and Troy nose to nose.

What's your problem? says Femi.

I ain't got a problem, says Troy.

Yes you have.

No I ain't.

We got to get out of here, you idiot! He fucked us once by bringing us here, now he done it again leaving us in the shit with a hostage, looking like it's all our fault! You think that's not a problem, you're sick in the head!

Who says he's gone? Who says he ain't coming back?

Femi steps back. Looks around. *Where is he, then?*

Troy don't budge and don't even blink. *Dunno, but I know he coming back. Matchstick's here. I'm here. The rest of us is here, so he's coming back.*

Says who?

You think he ain't, then you don't know him. You don't know nothing.

Well, stay if you want, 'cause I ain't.

Fine, but don't touch Matchstick.

Or what?

Just don't.

Then there's a voice from the zigzag doorway. Ain't even loud, but it cuts through like a shank, makes everyone spin to see what it is.

You got a problem with Matchstick?

It's Blaze.

I really got to be 110% focused. So I go to the doctor and he says here's some Ritalin. #determination

FEMI

You got a problem with Matchstick?

People talk about shitting yourself like it's a joke, like it's just words, but I swear when I hear that voice something goes—something loosens—and I ain't being funny, but if things had been different down there, I literally could have shit just like that, out of pure fear.

Can't show it, though, can I? That would just make me look worse. I know I just got to flip it—push things forward to try to make the Matchstick thing disappear. *Where you been?* I say, trying to sound angry instead of guilty or scared.

Out, he says. Like—big surprise. Why would he say anything else? And I know it's like a power thing—waiting for us all to dive in with, *What? where? why?*—but I ain't up for that. Why should I?

Where d'you go? says Lee. *We thought you'd done a runner.*

Who thought that? says Blaze.

Lee's eyes flick toward me, then away again. You can see him remembering that for him it's almost always a bad idea to open his mouth, 'cause something stupid always falls out.

Nobody, says Lee. *I mean, all of us. But just for a bit. I mean, we knew you'd be back soon. Didn't we?*

He's looking around for somebody to help him out, but nobody does.

Why didn't you say something? says Karen. *Instead of just going off.*

I sorted things out, he says. *We're leaving. After today. Last night tonight, then after that it's all over.*

What—the feds? You spoke to the feds? says Karen.

No.

So how d'you know what's happening tomorrow?

I don't.

But you said—

I just said it's ending. Don't know what it's going to be, but tomorrow it's ending. Something's going to happen and if it don't we just walk out. Okay?

Nobody says nothing. Nobody even nods. Only thing that moves is Matchstick appearing back out of the corner and shuffling up behind Blaze.

Thought we should celebrate, he says, and it's only then with him taking it off that I realize he's got a backpack on. He unzips it and takes out a speaker dock and two bottles of vodka. Smirnoff. The real thing. After that there's some spray paints. Then he tips the bag up and tons of sweets and stuff tumble out all over the floor.

Matchstick's looking right at me. There's poison in them little eyes of his and I got this sick feeling that even though I never told Blaze what happened—even though Blaze acted like he forgot the question he started with—what I did ain't going to be ignored.

But if it's all over tomorrow, then that's like some massive reset button that's just going to cancel everything that's happened before. Once the feds come in—or whoever it is—that's everything between me and Blaze and Matchstick wiped clean. But anyway, there's tons of vodka, and a whole afternoon and evening and night to get through before it's tomorrow, so anything could happen. I still feel jumpy, proper jumpy, knotted up and halfway to a puke.

Blaze walks away up to the office—leaves the bottles and the paint and the sweets and the speaker and just wanders off—no explanation, nothing. Karen goes up with him and we all sort of flop out. Nobody opens the vodka or puts on music or nothing. I mean, it's too early, maybe that's why. There's still food lying around, so we pick at yesterday's stuff and eat some sweets. After a bit, Lee goes for the paints and starts spraying walls and machines and things. Shaking and spraying. Just blotches and spirals and swear words. Nobody really watches or joins in. There's a moment when he goes still and tries to do what I think might be a cat or something, but he gives up and covers it over with a long squirt.

That's when I slip out. I mean, nobody's watching, so why not? Out the folding door. Through the bent metal wall flap. Across the warehouse. Up them stairs. Along the balcony. Try not to look down but can't not—just like last time. Up onto the windowsill, I swear, even a pigeon would feel weird up here, it just ain't right.

Crawl along. Out the window. Along the ledge. Pause at that corner where Blaze was hiding and this time I stop. Just peep around. Nothing there.

Keep going. Going and going. Another corner.

Then another.

And another.

Then I'm back where I started, ain't I?

No way out. No way down. Just this massive drop all the way around.

It was a setup. Whole thing was a setup.

So what can I do? What? Except go back in and sit around and wait to see what happens.

It's either that or jump off.

I kneel and look over the edge. Long way down. Tarmac. White lines at neat diagonals to fit in the right number of cars. It'd all be over in a moment. No consequences then— no explaining—nothing. It would only take a second. I can see which parking space I'd land in.

It's weird how you don't even choose who you become. Nobody ever tells you that when you're small. All this shit's just going to happen to you, and you're some tiny little insect that's flapping its wings hard as it can to try and get to where it wants to get to—but when the wind blows, it's the wind that's going to decide where you end up. Ain't you at all, however hard you flap them pissy little wings.

If it was up to me, I wouldn't never have met nobody like Blaze or Troy or any of them. I wouldn't have ended up with friends that ain't even friends. I wouldn't have ended up like this, all on my own up on some roof with no options, no choices, just boxed in on every side between different things that I don't want—that nobody would want.

I never hurt nobody. Never wanted to and never did.

Can't think of nothing now except Mum and Dad, and they come at me like faces out of a mist swirling all around. It's like I'm wrapped in them—like I'm up high on this tiny ledge and there's this sheet wrapping me tighter and tighter—but it ain't a sheet, it's Mum and Dad and what I done to them and how I messed everything up, and the guilt of it is choking me and swallowing me up, and I swear, even if I don't jump I might just fall, 'cause the power of it...the crush is so strong, it's like maximum

pain and no pain at all...at the same time...like when
light gets brighter and brighter until there's so much whiteness you can't see nothing at all...so bright it might as
well be pitch dark...same thing, I swear, I can feel everything and nothing almost like I'm dead already and just
floating away...squeezed so hard there ain't even nothing
left to squeeze...nothing...'cause the person that was me
ain't there anymore, he's just flown up...and whoever it is
on that ledge...swaying and wobbling...that ain't
me...and if he stays up or falls down, that don't even
make no difference to nobody...

It's the day of our Lord! Traditional celebration—snorting
Ritalin and shotgunning Bud.

Twitter

TROY

It's hours they're up there. Don't know what they're doing. I
mean, I do—but still—ain't right bringing all the vodka and
everything, then just disappearing so everyone else is hanging around waiting.

Afternoon trickles past, nothing happening—Matchstick stacking tires and knocking them over—Lee spraying
stuff—Femi off somewhere, don't know where—them
two at it upstairs—and me just sitting there. I swear, it
might as well be me that's the hostage—that's how bored
I am.

Eventually I go in to the guy. Take a Smirnoff. Ain't
opened yet, but I mean, what's stopping me—why should I
wait for them?

It's weird the way he looks up at me like not awake, not
asleep, but half of each. Skin around his eyes gone all red.
Under that gray with tiny lumps like a lizard or something. Mouth and cheeks look like they've sort of collapsed
in—almost like he's starving but he ain't, 'cause we fed
him and everything.

He looks at me but not scared like before—just kind of
wary and tired like he given up.

You want a drink? I say, holding out the vodka. Opening it.
Click click click, it goes with the seal breaking apart.

196

He hears me but it's like I ain't even spoken. He don't say nothing or shake his head or nod—it's like he don't even understand the language.

I stand there watching him—feeling the tiny sharp bumps on the rim of the lid around and around with my index finger—then I take a big gulp and I swear, it's so disgusting. Like gasoline or acid or I don't know what, just poison. I like the bit after it's out of your mouth though. The burn as it goes down. All them bits of your insides that you don't normally even know is there—you can feel them lighting up one by one as the voddie passes through. Then there's this afterglow in your mouth, a tingle a bit like pain, but not.

It's over, I say to him. *Tomorrow. All over.*

That makes him listen.

His eyes go small, then his mouth opens and he starts to talk, but the first thing that comes out ain't even a word. It's more like a grunt, I don't know what it is, but you can see he's as surprised as I am that his words ain't coming out how he wants. He stops a moment and tries again—but slow—like he's got used to the idea of being tied up and time just going nowhere and nothing ever needing to happen in a hurry 'cause there ain't anything going to happen anyway.

Are...you...serious? he says in a voice so slow it's almost funny but actually ain't.

It's horrible being in with him now. Just so depressing. Pitiful it is—the sight of him. He ain't playing no games now—trying to mess with me—figure out an escape—he ditched all that a while ago. Now he just sits there. Even after this is over I know his face is going to haunt me. It's what a person looks like when you strip out what it is that makes you alive. Or most of it. You can't see him without thinking how people and animals is almost the same—how if you take away the talk and the freedom to decide what to do—what's left ain't no better than a dog.

Ought to make you feel big. The power. The difference between me and him, it ought to make me feel like a king. Don't, though.

Can't figure out why Blaze wanted this. Can't figure it out.

Serious, I says. *This is the last night. Vodka?*

I hold out the bottle again—but hoping he won't reach out, 'cause then I'd have to go closer and I don't want to. Just want to get out of there.

He shakes his head and I leave.

Give the bottle to Lee. He takes a big swig. Screws up his mouth and eyes—looks almost like he's going to cry—but he gets it down.

Not exactly a party, is it—just me and Lee swigging this throat-scraping acid—tragic, more like—but eventually Blaze and Karen come down—lazy and loose like floating back to earth from their blissed-out cloud. Can't even look at that smile they got on their faces.

Blaze puts on some music and things get going. Femi turns up after that—weirdest look he got—like a ghost—reminds me of the hostage, I don't know, it's something in the eyes, something there but not there—and he don't say nothing, but he takes a bottle and gulps it like water. Keep on thinking he has to stop, but he don't. The amount he gets down, it's scary.

Then Lee's got the hostage walking around with him and he's on the rope almost like a dog and Lee's saying, *Let's paint him.*

Nobody even knows what he's talking about, but Lee just does it anyway. Lets go of the string and the guy don't run or do anything—he just stands there—and Lee gets a can of paint and starts spraying him white all over on top of his clothes. Not his face, but everywhere else. Gets another can and does another and another—yellow, then red, then black—then this danccy track comes on and I think the vodka must be hitting, 'cause soon we're all dancing—all of us around him in a circle—swirling around and around this weird painted man—and Karen starts shouting at him to dance—yelling in his face—it's weird, she must be out of it, but it don't make no difference—he don't dance. His legs sort of crumple under him and he falls to his knees—then Blaze takes him away and we put the music up even higher and the dancing turns into climbing up things and jumping off them and jumping all over each other and I can't stop thinking about how it's going to be over tomorrow and how that's just a massive relief. Don't know if it's the vodka or the relief that makes everyone go so mental.

Just gets wilder and wilder. Everyone chucking tires at each other and doing the weirdest, stupidest dancing you ever seen. Then Lee's on the balcony and he climbs up onto the railing right over the big drop with one hand on the wall to steady himself and he says, *Watch this,* and he takes his dick out and starts pissing. Piss sprays down everywhere and he's laughing and laughing, but nobody else is, and Karen's going, *THAT'S DISGUSTING, THAT'S DISGUSTING, YOU'RE SICK!* but he don't care and he keeps laughing and pissing until he slips. He's got one hand on a bit of metal that's sticking out the wall but now his legs are dangling on the wrong side of the railings and it's like an electric shock—one second you're out of it—next second you're just so alert running up them stairs—I'm the first and Blaze is right behind—but Femi's nowhere, he's passed out or something, and Karen's just screaming.

We get there—hold him around the waist—drag him back in—and it's horrible, 'cause his trousers are down and half covered in piss and he don't even know what's happened. He's still laughing and we just leave him there on the balcony with his pissy trousers down and everything. Don't want to touch him any more than we have to.

And that's that. Party vibe totally gone. I walk over and check that Femi's breathing and everything, which he is—then I just flop out. Feel like I probably need a piss or a puke or maybe both, but I can't be bothered. Just sort of drop down and zone out easy as flicking off a light.

There's a half thought floating around my head as I drift off—wondering where I'll be sleeping tomorrow—but I don't let it in. Or try not to, anyway. Plenty of time to worry about that later. All the time in the world.

It's good that we partied even if it ended bad. Last chance. Maybe ever.

Day Six

Stupid ex-husband turns up with Ethan and no Ritalin. Didn't give it to him all weekend. Typical. Now I have to deal with the fallout.

Twitter

THE NEGOTIATOR

When the call comes in, my first reaction is that they must be pulling my leg. Frankly, I have never heard anything so ludicrous. I try to explain that taking things in this direction is unnecessary, dangerous, jumping the gun, rash, unworkable, just not appropriate by any measure of prudent or competent policing whatsoever.

But do they listen to me? The suits? Of course not. These people who have never been face-to-face with an actual felon in their lives, they see fit to tell officers like my good self, with years of front-line work under the belt, how to resolve a situation. Decades of experience, and what does it count for up against some manicured nancy boy with a degree? Zip.

It's a strange conversation, though, because the guy who tells me what's going to happen doesn't seem to disagree about any of my objections. If I were required to summarize the conversation, I'd do it as follows:

1 – These are your orders.
2 – It's an atrocious idea, but it's what the mayor wants, so there's nothing we can do to stop him.
3 – Make sure he doesn't get killed.

The mayor has clearly sniffed out the political capital in an attempt at physical heroism, and it's our balls on the line (excuse the French) if it goes tits up (ditto).

The press must have been tipped off, because they all perk up and reappear carrying take-out coffee cups and microphones minutes before the mayor's car speeds into view. From the moment he steps out of his vehicle, the place becomes not so much a crime scene as a film premiere. The cameramen go wild, wanting shot after shot of him arriving. He doesn't exactly pose for them, but he doesn't not pose, either. He walks toward me as slowly as is humanly possible, pausing to look around like a mountaineer surveying the view from a summit, to guarantee that every photographer gets every shot they want from every possible angle.

Journalists fire questions at him, asking him to confirm or deny the rumor that he might be going into the warehouse. His people must have leaked the story, but that doesn't necessarily mean he won't deny it. If he's mad enough to be considering going in, he'll have some plan for how to milk it for maximum drama.

He doesn't answer any of the journalists until he's standing beside me. He silences the crowd with one raised hand. You can see by the half smirk at the corner of his mouth how much he enjoys the instant effect of that small gesture.

"I can't comment on those rumors," he says. "I haven't come here to talk; I've come to listen. We have some of London's finest, most experienced officers on the scene here, and I've come to see firsthand the excellent work they are doing, to hear more about the progress they are making, and if there is anything I can contribute to their fine efforts, I will of course do whatever I can. I hope to have more news for you soon."

With that, he turns and walks away from the baying press pack. He walks purposefully, but in no particular direction. I hurry to catch up with him.

"Where the hell am I going?" he mutters.

"Incident room's this way," I say, swerving him toward the small requisitioned office where we'll be able to talk in private. A vapor trail of minions follows behind, but only a couple are selected to attend our talk. They hover in the background, scowling at me, not with any particular hostility, more because they appear to have the kind of faces that only know how to scowl. It's the white-collar tough-guy look, which is to say not tough at all. Scowl back and they'd urinate.

The mayor sits, before I have offered him a seat.

"You haven't achieved anything here, have you?" he barks.

"We're making progress. Patience is of the essence in this kind of situation, for the safety of the hostage."

"Nonsense," he says. "We don't have time for that."

"These rumors. Are they true?"

"Of course they're bloody true. Why do you think I'm here? For a chat with you?"

"You want to go in and talk to the kidnappers? On your own?"

"I don't *want* to. But it's an opportunity that is simply too good to throw away, and these are the moments on which a career is built. So I'm going to do it."

"Why?"

"I've been assured you are a perfectly adequate policeman, but it's clear you know nothing about politics, which is fine, so let's just circumvent this entire debate. Just get me some gear. Bulletproof vest. Stab vest. Something like that. Something that can go over my suit jacket." His gaze suddenly shoots to the female minion. "Or shirt sleeves? What do you think? Jacket off?" She nods and he turns back to me. "Something with an aura of 'war zone' about it, but not so bulky that I look overcautious or afraid. Have you got something like that?"

"Before we get to the costume, I feel compelled to remind you that there are serious risks involved in what you're doing. If no officers go with you, and even if they do, we can't ensure your safety."

"They're kids. I'm the mayor. What are they going to do to me? Since when did everyone get so terrified of kids?"

"Kids are the worst kind. They have no moral compass, no self-control, and no idea of the consequences of their actions. I deal with these people on a daily basis and they're feral. Society means nothing to them. If you think you're safe, you are mistaken. They're not like us. They've had no proper parenting and they probably spent most of the last ten years skipping school. They don't know anything about anything, and they've never eaten a vegetable in their lives."

"Perhaps I should take them a zucchini. Would that help?"

"I just feel I have to strongly advise you against the course of action you are taking."

"You are approximately the hundredth person to say that to me, but if I have one skill, it is an ability to know what plays well on the news. When was the last time you saw a politician actually *do* something?"

"I didn't think that was your job."

"Precisely. And if I can do this, if I can go out there and show a bit of guts, take this fellow's challenge and run with it, I'm a bloody hero, aren't I? And how many other people in my party can say that?"

"What if they attempt to harm you?"

"It's a handful of teenagers with a pocketknife. It's not Al Qaeda. We need a bit of perspective here."

"It's very much against procedure to allow this."

"Everybody in the whole country has had enough of cowering away from these people and being pushed around by them. This is my chance to lead from the front. I know there's a risk, but it's a small one, and this is an opportunity that has to be grasped immediately, or it'll be gone. There's a once-in-a-lifetime political jackpot just sitting there for the taking, right now, and I can't let that go. I'd be mad to let it go. Now STFU and get me a bloody vest."

"STFU?"

"Shut the. You can figure out the rest."

I feel my face going puce. I know he is the mayor of London, but that's no excuse for language. Luckily I am a man who possesses quite supreme self-control, because at this instant I am livid. Few things make me as angry as being spoken to with this combination of lewdness and arrogance. Nobody has made me this furious for years, except perhaps my son, my wife, my ex-wife, and my mother-in-law. There's also my ex-mother-in-law, traffic wardens, asylum seekers, and benefits scroungers, but apart from that, rage of this sort is a quite unfamiliar sensation to me.

If the population at large knew what politicians are really like, there'd be riots on the streets. Of course, there already are riots on the streets, but I'm referring to a different kind of riot. Different rioters, educated ones, rioting with good reason at the vanity and pomposity of the class of people elected to serve us.

Under provocation like this, the Dalai Lama himself would probably blow his top and chin the bastard, but I take a couple of deep breaths and do what I can to maintain my professional demeanor.

"Well, you've clearly made your decision," I huff, my tone of voice making it clear that he has very much lost my vote. For good. "I'll get you a stab vest. I suggest that once you're inside, you stay close to a window. The snipers will try and cover you." This is the first thing I've said that has penetrated the carapace of his ego. There's something about the word *sniper* that always wakes people up.

He takes the vest. There's some debate about whether or not to go tieless, and after assessing both looks, it is agreed that an open neck goes best with the body armor. Following a quick check of the hair in a minion's hand mirror, he turns and without even a word of thanks heads out.

This man is either slightly crazy or very, very ambitious— or, more likely, both. Perhaps the two are indivisible.

The press pack have been herded into a new spot, one that will give them a good wide shot of the mayor's solo walk into the warehouse. He strides toward them, but I don't go with him. I can't bear to hear another word seep out of that supercilious, scatological orifice. I am a tolerant man, but I simply cannot abide language.

I gaened so meny twiter folwers superfast since i started on
"ritalin"!! million thanx to u peRfornance enhancer druges :)

Twitter

LEE

the pain of it's unbelievable
   my head, I mean, just *BOOM BOOM BOOM,* throbbing
like you wouldn't believe
   don't even know what happened, but I swear my trousers
reek
   I'm on lookout
   somebody's got to be, and it's always me, which ain't
fair but
   a guy walks up
   don't look like a fed
   I seen him before on TV or something
   Femi does some, but not as much as me
   it's that hair, I seen it before
   Matchstick says he ain't tall enough to see out the window
but he could stand on a box, couldn't he?
   what's wrong with a box?
   definitely recognize him
   don't know why it's always me, it ain't fair and it's roasting
up here
   he's that bloke politics or something
   walking right toward us
   ain't fair Troy don't never do it

don't know why it's never his turn

it's piss, that's what the smell is

yesterday's piss kind of turning sweeter in the heat as the day goes on

he's like right up at the door and I'm thinking I know who this is and he's walking right in just like that

but not sweet like a cake or something

sweet in a ripe acid pukey way

Karen don't do it, neither, I have weird dreams about her, but I reckon everyone does, I mean, she's so awesome

I wouldn't ever do nothing because Blaze would kill me and I don't reckon she's into me or anything, but that don't mean I can't have dreams, sort of porno dreams, no harm in it, is there?

he's walking in!

that's when I think, *I'm the lookout!*

shit!

I'm not just supposed to look, I'm supposed to do something!

shit!

and he just like walked in and I'm too late, shit, I got to do something about it

shit

and I seen him before, I know I have

TROY

Nobody knows how he did it. It's not like he said anything
or told us what he'd figured out. Then one minute we're
just hanging like normal—and nothing seems to be going
on—but the door opens and there's footsteps and suddenly
we're all up on our feet thinking it's the feds coming in to
bust us, but it ain't. It's just one guy. The mayor. The fucking mayor.

Everyone just stares, then Lee comes in screaming his
head off until he sees he's too late—the guy's in already. He
stops shouting for a second then says, *It's him! Wassisname!*
Then Lee realizes there's no point 'cause he's miles behind
as usual, and he shuts up.

Blaze comes up to me—turns his back on the others—
and hands me something. It's his phone.

Video it, he says quiet in my ear, *but not so he notices. Start when he's sitting.*

I nod, but Blaze don't even see 'cause he's already gone over to the mayor.

Where's the girl? The journalist? says Blaze, not in the way you'd think you should talk to the mayor or someone like that—just totally straight and normal, not impressed or nothing. He's not disrespecting him, but he ain't respecting him, neither.

She couldn't come, he says—and it's weird 'cause it's the exact same voice as on TV and the exact same face and everything—but just having it right there in front of you in the real world is sort of mental, like it's Harry Potter or Buzz Lightyear or something—alive in the same room having a conversation. Just don't seem real. Part of me wants to poke him with a finger to check.

Blaze don't seem freaked or nothing, though—'cause he just says, *Bullshit. I ain't talking without her here.*

You can see the mayor wasn't expecting that. He flinches and shuffles like he only just realized for the first time that it ain't going to be all pleases and thank-yous in here like what he's used to. *Let me explain. There's a reason,* he says. His voice is already less cocky—less TV smooth.

Don't bullshit me.

If you want me to help you—

Don't bullshit me.

Please, says the mayor—his eyes flicking toward the door like he's having second thoughts already and wondering whether to just run for it. *If we're going to do some kind of deal, there are some things I can only say in private. Away from journalists. Do you understand?*

Not really.

What I can say and what I can be seen to say are two different things.

Blaze stares at him with sideways eyes. *Let's sit down,* he says after a long gap.

First I need to see the hostage. Check that he's okay.

You can see him, but you can't talk to him.

The mayor nods and Blaze leads him away. There's a weird vibe after they've gone, like the place where the mayor was standing is a ticking bomb that's going to blow up any second. We all just stand there, not moving, not saying nothing, just staring at the empty space. Femi looks at me and he still don't speak, but does like a silent shout with just his lips saying, *WHAT THE FUCK!?*

Did Blaze know he was coming? says Karen, looking at me.

I shrug. *Dunno. Looks like it.*

I'm freaking? says Karen. *I'm so freaking right now.*

That's the mayor, ain't it? says Lee.

'Course it is, you shitwad, says Femi. *Who d'you think it was?*

Lee's face shrinks embarrassed but trying to cover it. *I'm just saying...*

So thick, man.

You are.

You are.

They're coming back, I say.

We go quiet and just stand there while the footsteps get closer. There's no talking, just the shuffle of shoes on concrete. The mayor's got them fancy heels that click-clack with each step, like an early warning system to let everyone know what a dick you are before you even arrive.

They sit—the mayor looking proper nervous now—you can tell the sight of his guy tied to a radiator has freaked him out. He looks all around the room like he's checking nobody's hiding, ready to jump him—and after he's sat, he shuffles his chair nearer to the window.

What you doing? says Blaze.

The mayor stops shifting around. *Just getting comfortable,* he says through tight lips and trying to smile, but it ain't even close to a real one—it's more like what you do just before you puke. Blaze gives me a quick look, but he don't need to, 'cause I already got the video running—held in one hand near my waist so it don't look like I'm doing nothing. Just a half nod and Blaze knows I'm on it.

I didn't think you'd come, says Blaze.

Nobody thought I'd come. But I took the view that I'm sure you are reasonable people who can be negotiated with in a way that leads this to a peaceful outcome.

Bullshit, you're bullshitting me. Only language you speak, ain't it?

Why else would I come?

For yourself.

I'm not the issue here.

Says who?

There's a hostage in this building. A member of my staff. I'm here to get him out.

Yeah, but first I need to know if you can speak any language other than bullshit, and it looks like you can't.

That may be your opinion, and you're entitled to it, but let's talk about the hostage. We'd all like to get him safely released, yet you don't appear to have issued any demands. What is it you want?

You ain't here for him, you're here for yourself.

I think we need to try and get less side-tracked here.

You can have him.

I beg your pardon?

You can have him back. We don't want him no more.

You mean... now?

Yeah. Why not? But we need a couple of things. There's no way we're all getting off, is there?

I'm afraid that's not possible.

Then it's gotta be just me. You got it on security cameras, ain't you? When we took him? You can see it's just me that done this. The others ain't done nothing. I made them come here.

That ain't true! I shout. Don't know why, but I'm almost crying. Seriously, almost. The tears are right there just ready to spring out, 'cause I know that whatever I do, Blaze is going to make this happen and it's all going to fall on him.

Shut it, Troy, he snaps—not loud, but proper angry.

Why are you doing this?

I said shut it.

I look at Karen, wanting her to speak up, but she's just looking at the floor, not saying nothing—and you can see on her face that she wants it. Anything that gets her off is fine by her, whatever happens to Blaze. I always knew she was like that—always knew she wasn't for real, and now here's the proof.

I think we could arrange that, says the mayor—his voice juiced up with how pleased he is, but trying to hide it.

Then we got a deal, says Blaze, reaching out to shake his hand. The mayor—his cheeks all rosy and puffed like he just ate a big fat pie—stretches to shake, but just before they do, Blaze pulls his hand back.

And there's something else, he says. *'Cause you're the dick here, ain't you?*

If we have a deal, you can call me whatever you like.

I said there's something else before we got a deal. Can't have you walking out the hero, can we? That ain't right.

This has nothing to do with me.

Bullshit. You got to pay a price, too. What about the hair?

What about it?

Off.

I beg your pardon?

Karen here's a trainee beautician. She'll do a good job.

What are you talking about?

All off. Shaved. That's the deal.

This is ludicrous.

That's the deal. You take the haircut, you walk out of here with the hostage. Straight after. You don't—the deal's off.

I've never heard such nonsense! I'm not doing that!

And we got it on video.

Pardon?

This conversation. We got it on video.

Blaze nods toward me. The mayor's head spins. I turn the screen and show him that I'm recording.

So if you don't do it, we can have this up on YouTube in a few minutes and everyone'll know that you had a deal but you wouldn't take it 'cause you didn't want a haircut.

That's absurd!

It is pretty fucked up, ain't it?

I'm the elected mayor of this city. If you think you can corner me with some kind of schoolboy prank like this…you…you…

We what? says Blaze—oh man, he's smiling now; I ain't never seen him smile so big.

If you think I'm falling for this…

Deal's off? You don't want it?

I didn't say that. I'm just saying we should negotiate like adults.

But I ain't an adult. I'll give you a minute to make up your mind.

This is like Who Wants to Be a Millionaire? says Femi, almost shaking, he's finding it so funny. *Ask him if he wants to phone a friend.*

He ain't got a friend! says Lee—all squeaky and high—hopping like a kid who needs a piss.

Blaze ignores them and eyeballs the mayor.

What's wrong with you? says the mayor—spitting the words out—angry now, so angry it almost ain't even funny.

I'm ill, ain't I? says Blaze, heavy sarcastic. *Sick in the head. We all are.*

Well, evidently that's the case.

That's why we all been on them pills since we was small. Us and every other kid in the projects that don't cut it at school.

Is that what this is about? I thought the police sent in a supply.

Burned it. Don't want that shit no more.

What are you saying?

I'm saying you got no respect for us. None of us. You want us to disappear. And since you can't do that, the next best thing is to just shut us up, ain't it? Soften us up, calm us down, keep us quiet and out the way where we won't 'cause trouble.

I've never instituted any policy that wasn't for the good of London as a whole. Nobody has forced anybody to take anything they didn't choose to take.

Paying parents to drug their kids? You think that's okay? You been doing it for so long you can't even see how sick it is.

That is an utterly perverse reading of the policy.

We ain't ill. We're just inconvenient.

Mental health professionals of an extremely high standing—

Minute's up, says Blaze—cutting him off without even raising his voice. He never needs to shout—don't know how, he just doesn't. *Decision time. You in or you out?*

The mayor stares at him—jaw slack and eyes empty—like a guy that's just taken a punch.

2013 was a strong year for Shire...Guidance for 2014 was also robust with management forecasting product sales growth 'in the mid-to-high teens' and earnings to grow at a similar rate to 2013 (20%+)...Shire's positioning in the fast growing ADHD market is the key reason for our positive view on the stock. ADHD has become big business in the US, driven by the launch of new products with improved properties and reduced potential for abuse...Shire believes there is still significant untapped potential in the adult market though, as its penetration rate of 40% is still far below the 75—80% penetration rate in the paediatric market.

www.barclaysstockbrokers.co.uk/Market-Insight/Analysis/Pages/share-of-the-week.aspx 3/3/2014

THE HOSTAGE

Dead or crazy. Dead or crazy. It must be one of the two and I can't even tell which. It's days now since I slept. I've grabbed snatches, but if anything, the terror's even worse in my sleep, and with the cord around my wrist I can't get comfortable, so there's hardly any point. And they keep coming in to look at me. All of them, one after the other, just wandering in to stare or gloat or I don't know what.

You'd think it would be obvious when it's day and when it's night, because I can see the sunlight streaking in, but the night doesn't really feel like night, I don't know why, it all just feels like one long stretch of time with no markers, no pauses, nothing—just an endless now drifting on and on.

I feel as if it's late, as if it might be the middle of the night, when they drag me out. First time ever apart from toilet stops that they've untied me from the radiator. They're drunk or high or something. There's a wildness that's new and unnerving and for a moment I think maybe it's a dream or a hallucination, because these creatures around me are talking to me, shouting at me, and I can hear the words but also not hear. I can't make out what they're saying to me. I can just hear music—strange, diabolical, repetitive dance music like some psychotic, wayward heartbeat—then one of them gets out a spray can and shakes it up. Even though their voices seem distant and indistinct, the rattle of the ball bearing inside the can pierces through me as if it's my own skull that is being shaken. The boy's eyes are glassy, swimming, tiny pinpricks of savagery and threat.

It's when he starts painting me that I begin to doubt what I'm seeing, doubt what is happening, doubt my sanity. I get a strong sense this can't be me—I can't be this object being sprayed in paint. Even though the acrid smell from the aerosol is burrowing up my nostrils, needling into my lungs, I feel sure I can't actually be in this place among those people with these events taking place. I must be somewhere else. I don't know where, or what my connection is to the body in the warehouse; I just know that the humiliated, graffitied, human-shaped object in the middle of this warehouse, surrounded by crazed, bloodthirsty thugs, can't be me.

Though at the same time I know it is.

And isn't.

So the only explanation is that I'm losing my mind or have lost my mind or my mind has lost me.

More cans. Rattle shake rattle shake *fshhhhhhhhhhhhhhhhhhh.* On my legs, my chest, my arms and hair. *Fssshhhhhhhhhhhhhhhhhh!* Like a steam train cooling at the end of a journey. Like being erased.

It can't be me. That cannot be my body white and yellow and red and black—and then they're even closer all around me and the music's even louder now—not even music—just a brutal tooth-rattling beat—and I realize the girl is telling me to dance. Poking me. Kicking me. Her face is young and pure and beautiful and also wizened and demonic and hideous. Her voice is saying, *DANCE! DANCE! DANCE, YOU PRICK!*

I don't hear the words, I see them. Metal spirals coming out of her mouth. Just hatred and savagery and scorn, molten, forged into coils that fly toward me through the air—darts too strange and twisted to fly, but they do—out of her mouth and into me—snipping the veins, the muscles, the nerves and tendons—unraveling the knots that hold me in one piece—because I know then that I am falling and maybe dissolving. I cannot stand and I cannot think and I cannot speak, so I must be asleep or crazy or dead and these creatures taunting me cannot be there. Perhaps I'm free already. Perhaps I am in a hospital bed somewhere. Perhaps I am dead or half-dead or dying.

But then they've gone and I'm tied to the radiator again and I think I'm awake, so I suppose I've just woken up, but there's still the smell—that sweet ammoniac smell—and my arms crackle when I move and—yes—I've been painted. I have been painted.

So perhaps I haven't woken up at all, because next thing the mayor's in there, so I just laugh at him because it's so stupid and he asks me if I'm okay, and I just say, *Yeah, I'm fine, I'm having the time of my life,* because I mean, what's the point in even taking this conversation seriously when it can't possibly be happening, though there's something in the shock and horror on his face that looks a bit too real.

But too real for what? I don't even care anymore. I'm so tired.

He goes. I think he does. Then he comes back. At least, a version of him comes back. And that's when I know for sure that I've cracked. The sight of him. I don't know whether to scream or laugh.

Calling all RTC students! In school tomorrow I'm selling Ritalin.
Look for the guy in a red polo and Lakers cap.

Twitter

KAREN

So mental? Like, beyond mental? Like, I don't have the words? To describe it? And when the mayor says yes I'm like, *Oh, shit,* and like, *But I don't have no scissors!* Then Blaze says there's a pair in the drawer of the desk in the office where we been boning, and I don't know how he knows, but there's no point in asking yourself that when it's Blaze, 'cause he knows stuff, he just does, and it's not worth even trying to figure out how.

I'm just like too weirded out by the whole thing? To get the scissors? I'm flipping out, but then Matchstick's standing there right next to me with that freaky look on his face, and he's holding out the scissors?

That ain't scissors! I scream, stressing badly. I mean, they're like totally old? And rusty? And not even hair scissors but paper scissors, which is a totally different thing? Obviously? I take them off him anyway—to try and explain—and as soon as I touch the blades I'm just like totally, *No way!*

Blunt isn't even the word for how blunt they are. I mean, I been training to do this properly for months with proper equipment, and I can't just do a haircut with scissors that ain't even proper scissors, specially when it's on someone *famous!* I mean, everyone's going to see it! I only ever done models so far, and they do it for the free cut, 'cause the stylist comes after and finishes off and gets rid of the mistakes? I mean, they get a proper cut in the end. So no one's even seen a finished cut that I done all by myself, not once, not even one time. Then this is like someone famous? And there's TV cameras outside waiting for him? Waiting for him to come out? With my haircut? On TV?

It is scissors, says Troy. So smug? Like he's the expert? Like he's the one that knows about scissors when so obviously he ain't. Such a dick! 'Cause if he thinks he's being the clever one right now....

NOT HAIR SCISSORS! I say, trying to sound calm, but it comes out as a sort of shriek, which ain't my fault 'cause Troy just drives me crazy when he's all cocky. Everyone knows if it weren't for Blaze he'd just have to hide in the corner and disappear. *IT'S A TOTALLY DIFFERENT THING!*

I'll do it if you won't, says Blaze, totally casual, as if it ain't even nothing, as if this isn't, like, THE MOST IMPORTANT HAIRCUT EVER!

No way? I can do it!

I don't know how he changed my mind, but he did? One minute you want...I don't know...something...then Blaze speaks up and suddenly you want the opposite? He does that to people all the time.

Go on then, says Troy. That boy so needs a slap.

I open and close the blades a couple of times. They're stiff. Like, your worst nightmare?

We got any oil? I say.

Yeah, I always carry some with me, says Troy, but I just ignore him, 'cause actually that's the only way.

You can get some out of Lee's hair, says Femi.

Fuck off, says Lee, punching Femi proper hard, so he does it back, but after that they stop, probably because the mayor's right there.

I look down at him in his chair, dressed in his dorky shirt, looking flustered. He's so not happy. Big-time. Face like he's swallowed a dump.

It's the first time I ever actually touched someone from off the TV. I mean, someone I've seen, like, on the news and shit, but now he's right in front of me, and I'm reaching out, and I'm lifting up a tuft of his batty hair, and it's in my hands, proper real. It's freaky.

That first snip? And a little blond flake drifts down? Lands on my shoe? That's...like...unreal? I mean, actually cutting the mayor's hair! Actually famous hair? Then I'm cutting deeper in and the tufts falling down are chunkier and he's just looking more and more pissed off? And it turns out he's got a little bald patch at the back, so maybe that's why he has to keep it long? To cover it up?

And once I'm up and running, even though they're the worst scissors ever—I mean, my aunt would flip if she saw what I was using, 'cause you've got to be professional, that's what she's always telling me—even though it's the weirdest situation, after a bit I actually kind of enjoy it? Like, a power thing? I mean, this is the guy that runs the city? And everyone's heard of him? But it's me cutting his hair and he's just sitting there and taking it, even though he don't even want it cut. Like, the actual mayor? And the more I cut off, the worse he looks, which is so funny, but I got to stay on it, 'cause, like I say, you have to be professional.

Even with proper scissors you can't take it all off. Not without clippers? So nobody's going to judge me. It ain't even supposed to look good—that ain't the point of it—so I can't mess it up whatever I do, 'cause it's supposed to be messed up. The point is it's my cut.

He's going to be on the news and before the end of the day it'll be the most famous haircut in the world and it'll be me that done it. I ain't getting ideas or nothing, I know I'm still a trainee, but how many stylists in the world can say that? Like, none?

METHODS: Using Swedish national registers, we gathered information on 25,656 patients with a diagnosis of ADHD, their pharmacologic treatment, and subsequent criminal convictions in Sweden from 2006 through 2009...

RESULTS: As compared with nonmedication periods, among patients receiving ADHD medication, there was a significant reduction of 32% in the criminality rate for men...and 41% for women...

CONCLUSIONS: Among patients with ADHD, rates of criminality were lower during periods when they were receiving ADHD medication. These findings raise the possibility that the use of medication reduces the risk of criminality among patients with ADHD.

Lichtenstein P., Halldner L., Zetterqvist J., Sjölander A., Serlachius E., Fazel S., Långström N., Larsson H., "Medication for attention deficit-hyperactivity disorder and criminality," *New England Journal of Medicine*

FEMI

So weird, the sight of it. Head skin. It ought not to be, 'cause lots of people's bald, but when it's someone that ain't bald, then you cut it off, it's like you stripped them naked. He looks such a freak. And his face is so pissed off it's almost the funniest thing you ever seen, except that as soon as it's finished there's no time to stop and look at it or laugh or anything like that, 'cause he just goes straight off to the hostage.

There's a moment when we're all looking at each other— or all looking at Blaze, anyway—but nobody moves till the mayor comes out with the guy, who's all limping and hunched and still painted, just the maddest-looking person I ever seen.

They go right past without looking at us, 'cause maybe they think we're going to stop them or change our mind or something. It's almost like they're trying to pretend we ain't there, which is a bit thick if you think about it.

Blaze don't speak or stop them or nothing, but after they gone past he walks right behind them. He ain't hiding or skulking—his body's almost saying he's the boss bringing these two weird-looking guys to the outside world.

Then we're alone again, but minus Blaze.

I can hear this sound, almost a roar or something from outside when all the people that's waiting see who's come out.

Run for it, man, says Troy, and he takes off out the front door. Matchstick's right behind, then me, and I can hear Lee and Karen following after.

Don't even make sense at first what I see out there—crowds of people behind a line of yellow tape staring at the three who's come out ahead of us, half of them taking photos. Troy ain't followed them, he's trying to run around the side, away from the feds, so I go after him, but it's seconds before they're all over us like ants, pushing us to the ground and cuffing us. Three guys lift me up and I can see Karen on the ground fighting the feds who's cuffing her, and she's screaming, *I AIN'T DONE NOTHING! I DONE THE HAIRCUT, BUT I AIN'T DONE NOTHING ELSE! I DONE NOTHING!*

They shove me toward some fed vans and I can see the mayor talking into hundreds of microphones spouting some bullshit, I don't know what, and Blaze is being dragged away in front of me. He's pointing at me and the others and shouting, *WE HAD A DEAL! WE HAD A FUCKING DEAL, YOU SCUMBAG! A DEAL!*

So intense, man, I can't take it all in, and I'm almost thinking this must be a film or TV or just not real, then near the van I see something that flips the whole situation and changes everything. It's Mum and Dad. They're behind the tape, at the front of the crowd, and they're staring right at me, and the look on their faces is like cold steel across my throat.

Never knew they'd be here. Never thought they'd watch me being cuffed and arrested. Never thought I would ever see them look at me with such horror and anger and sorrow lasering out of their eyes—so much it almost burns through me, shrivels my insides to just a pile of burned-up crumbs.

MUUUUUUUM! I shout. *MUUUUUUUM!* She hears me and our eyes lock for a second, but it's like she don't even recognize me. It's like she's saying, *Who are you? You ain't my boy!*

I want to shout to her that it is me, that I don't know what happened, that I didn't choose none of it. I just been weak, that's all. Weak and stupid, but I'm still me and I ain't bad or violent or sick in the head. I'm still her boy, and I don't want to be nothing else, but the police are pulling on me, dragging me off, and it takes more of them now 'cause my whole body's gone limp. Then I'm in the van.

Troy and Lee's already in there and the doors slam and the siren goes on. There's bangs on the side and we edge away slow at first, then suddenly proper fast. Troy's silent, but Lee's going on and on, saying, *I ain't done nothing, it wasn't my fault, it was Blaze.* It's stupid, pointless shit he's saying, but I got to block out what I'm thinking, so I start doing it, too, telling the feds that I never even touched the hostage and none of us hurt him and Blaze did it all, we was just watching, we was stuck there same as the hostage was.

Waste of breath, though, 'cause there's two feds in the back with us and they ain't even listening. One of them tries to calm Lee down, saying he can make a statement at the station, but Lee just gets more and more agitated until he punches the side of the van. After that he swears a bit 'cause he hurt himself, then he shuts up, so I do, too.

Soon as I stop yelling those two faces come back. Mum and Dad. Faces I known all my life—loved all my life—pulled into an expression I never saw before and never want to see again.

No use pretending otherwise, after everything they done for me, after what they went through to get to this country, I crushed the life out of them by doing what I done. They suffered like I can't hardly even imagine, put their hopes in me, now I just chucked it all away without even meaning to.

I had my chance up on the roof. I could've ended it all then and that might have been less bad than what I done to them now.

Can't even imagine where they're taking me, what's going to happen next. All I can think of is Mum and Dad—picturing them at home all the time I'm going to be in jail—waiting and waiting—going more and more dead every day, every week, every month, every year.

And after I come out, they ain't going to want me or trust me or even like me. There ain't going to be no connection between me and them or me and anyone else. I'm just going to be alone. Rest of my life.

What's the point of even locking me up? Might as well just bury me, 'cause I ain't even alive no more. I really ain't.

The van's going left, right, left through the traffic just like normal, but there's no windows and I get the weirdest feeling. Ain't like the van's going forward at all. Not backward, neither. I can feel in my chest and my heart and my legs what's really happening 'cause that van it's more like an elevator, and we're going down and down and down. Straight down. Stop for a bit at traffic lights. Then off we go again. Down and down.

A Brazilian team of researchers calculated...that hyperactivity occurred in 5.29 per cent of the world's childhood population...as explained...in the *American Journal of Psychiatry*. According to the commentary which accompanied the article, such findings gave weight to the status of the disorder's 'identity as a bona fide mental disorder'...and weakened assertions that hyperactivity was a 'fraud propagated by the profit-dependent pharmaceutical industry'...This was despite the fact that the study itself was funded in part by pharmaceutical company Eli Lilly, for whom one of the authors, Silva de Lima, works as medical director. Two of the other authors were on the board of Eli Lilly and had ties to many other pharmaceutical companies, receiving funding from them and serving on their speakers' bureaus.

Matthew Smith, *Hyperactive: The Controversial History of ADHD*

THE JOURNALIST

I was hardly surprised that the mayor cut me out of the meeting with Blaze. It was the walk in and the walk out that was the story. There wasn't anything to be gained for him by having his conversation with the kids reported. If he went in alone, he could spin the meeting however he wanted. Plus, it was a visual thing. The walk into the warehouse, facing down danger, the brave maverick peacemaker, that's what he was selling. I would have spoiled the pictures.

The politics editor was the only one who guessed he might go in. The mayor wouldn't even have to achieve anything by it. If he could just cross the no-man's-land in front of the police lines, get through those doors, then walk out again after longer than a couple of minutes, his image would be transformed forever. He'd have something the PM wouldn't be able to buy with a million-quid advertising campaign. If he could pull it off, he might begin to look like…well, a man. Once and for all, he'd draw a line between himself and the pampered, lily-livered wimps that constitute the rest of his party. For Hugo Nelson, that was an irresistible prize.

So when he comes out, even though it's my story that set the whole thing up, I'm just part of the crush along with every other journalist in the Western hemisphere. Cameras clack frantically the moment the warehouse door slides open, but it takes us a second or two to realize what we are seeing. When we do, a surge of hysterical amazement sweeps through the crowd.

First out is the mayor, alongside an ill-shaven thirtyish white guy who blinks in the light and staggers as if his legs are barely strong enough to carry him. It's the hostage. He's wearing what at first looks like a lurid suit, but as they get closer, it becomes apparent that he seems to have been spray-painted. Graffitied. The mayor, perhaps remembering how scenes like this are supposed to look in movies, takes the hostage's arm and pulls it across his shoulders. Together, they stumble forward.

But it's not the sight of the hostage that gets people staring in disbelief. It's the mayor's hair. Or, rather, lack of it. The whole lot has been cut off. Apart from a few straggly tufts above his ears, every strand of that famous blond hair has been hacked off, which perhaps explains the look of dazed uncertainty on his face, poised somewhere between, "This is the greatest triumph of my political life," and, "Never before have I looked more of a prick."

Directly behind the mayor and the hostage is Blaze, head held high in a posture of swaggering defiance. A second or two after Blaze comes into view, five other kids, four boys and a girl, emerge at a sprint. Unlike Blaze, they don't follow the mayor but attempt to run around the side of the building. This kicks the police into action. A swarm of them sprint toward the kids, catching them within seconds and shoving them to the ground.

Blaze doesn't attempt to run away, but he is also pushed to the concrete, patted down and cuffed. He seems calm, oddly detached from what is happening to him, but when he sees what the police do to the other five, he starts shouting and thrashing.

The other kids yell and struggle as they're shoved into police vans and driven away. The mayor ignores the kerfuffle behind him and walks toward the TV cameras, still supporting the weight of the hostage. To the side I notice a paramedic edge toward them, but the mayor grips the rescued man's arm. He isn't letting go just yet.

He clears his throat. "Ladies and gentlemen of the press," he says. "It is with immense relief that I stand here, knowing I have managed to negotiate an end to this appalling kidnap. Mr. Paxton has shown immense courage throughout his ordeal, and I'm pleased to report that he is in good health and looking forward to reuniting with his family. For myself, you... you may have noticed a slight change in my appearance. Well, these children, these exemplars of the feral youth who have been allowed to terrorize the honest people of this country for far too long, insisted on extracting their pound of flesh. Or hair. Perhaps they thought this would constitute some kind of revenge, or humiliation. Well, I may get it neatened up a little, but I plan to keep my hair in this style, not as a badge of humiliation, but as a badge of pride. Pride that I will not be intimidated by the lurid aggression of today's youth. Pride that I intend, for the rest of my political career, to stand up to these people and face down this problem once and for all. It is time for a little less understanding, and a little more punishment. If you'll excuse me, this has been a challenging day. I shall be taking questions tomorrow."

As his car drives away, a sense pervades the crowd that we have witnessed the defining moment in the career of a future prime minister.

The editor orders me back to the office, not to file, but to celebrate. This is sure to be the story of the year. Everyone involved is expected for drinks after work. A glass of wine in his office for a select few, then, no doubt, a general exodus to the pub.

In the course of the evening, I discover that yearning for recognition and praise does not, to my surprise, produce the ability to enjoy them when they arrive. If my ego had been commissioned to script a shamelessly self-glorifying scenario, this gathering would have been it. The editor is so effusive with his compliments, I'm almost embarrassed. Colleagues who've been ignoring me for years buy me drinks I haven't even asked for. I seem to have acquired an aura of temporary celebrity, with everyone wanting to greet or congratulate me.

They may well all be insulting me behind my back— they are journalists, after all—but being on the receiving end of admiration (and even just civility) feels like a transformation of my fortunes. Yet I don't truly enjoy one moment of it. I feel fraudulent, insincere, and guilty—not because my career fillip is undeserved, but because the whole enterprise, and the glory associated with it, feels corrupt.

I can't forget Blaze. While I'm being toasted and feted, he is in a cell. I can't forget what he was shouting to the mayor: "We had a deal. We had a deal."

Nobody else seems to have noticed this, or wondered what that deal might have been. There was no mention of it in any news reports. Blaze and his gang have been portrayed as ruthless thugs deserving of the most severe punishment.

The vague, inchoate menace that has been terrorizing the city now has a name and a face and a physical body on whom punishment and retribution can be heaped. Meanwhile, Hugo Nelson seems to have emerged with a burnished halo.

Even though it's not too late for the trains, I treat myself to a taxi home. Exhaustion and alcohol knock me out during the journey. The taxi driver has to wake me up outside my apartment.

But I don't go to bed. Foggy-headed and nauseous, I head for my laptop.

A new idea is dimly tingling at the back of my skull. It doesn't have a shape yet, but it's something to do with Professor Pyle—it's the puzzle of his sleek, glossy institute and his sleek, glossy secretary. The place has a style that doesn't fit with either academia or government. It was built with real money. But whose?

There is, of course, a sleek and glossy website—page after page of text reveling in the manifold achievements of the institute, artfully interspersed with photographs of central-casting scientist types contemplating arrays of research hardware, all against a hygienic white background—but nowhere any mention of who is funding the place.

Pyle's name is all over the Web. Even filtering results to articles written by him produces an unwieldy mass of material. I plod through, looking for clues as to who is paying for the Pyle Mercedes, but there's nothing.

It's two in the morning, and I'm on the brink of giving up, when I part with my credit card details for a pay-walled academic paper search engine and library. His most cited article comes up first. It's a piece of research connecting ADHD medication to lowered rates of criminality, whose title I've seen sprinkled across the Web. It is on this work that his reputation appears to be built, and from this reputation that his government appointment was won.

A small footnote at the end states that the research was funded by GlobExxoPharm. A few clicks later, I've confirmed that GlobExxoPharm are the makers of Concentr8. I'm suddenly wide awake.

I have another story. The biggest one yet. If Pyle was successfully recommending to the government the widespread prescription of Concentr8, while also being on the payroll of the company that makes the drug, that makes for a gold-plated, copper-bottomed scandal.

The unjustified drugging of large numbers of children struck me as a pretty good scandal a few days ago, but even now that is fading away in the public consciousness, replaced by the gaudier thrills of the hostage crisis and the mayor's pseudo-heroics. The world at large does not, it appears, care all that much about which drugs are administered to disaffected children. But this is a scandal about money. And you don't need a journalism degree to know that if you want to get people's attention, there's no better subject.

My fingers are trembling with excitement as I go over the facts once more, checking I haven't made a mistake.

It's watertight. Hugo Nelson had better enjoy his glory while he can, because as soon as this is out, he's finished.

As Grassley's investigation unfolded, he exposed more and more psychiatrists for similar infringements. Some of the more prominent culprits included Joseph Biederman of Massachusetts General Hospital (colloquially known as the 'King of Ritalin'), who was reported to have earned $1.6 million in consulting fees from drug companies between 2000 and 2007, most of which was not disclosed to Harvard University officials. There was also Dr Frederick Goodwin, former director of the National Institute of Mental Health, no less. He was reported to have earned at least $1.3 million between 2000 and 2007 for marketing lectures to physicians on behalf of drug companies. He did not disclose this to relevant parties such as national media outlets, where he'd been invited to speak publicly about drugs.

James Davies, *Cracked: Why Psychiatry Is Doing More Harm Than Good*

TROY

Ain't never quiet here. Middle of the night now and there's banging and shouting from the other cells on and on. Don't make no difference anyway—'cause even if there was a luxy bed and soft sheets and total silence I'd still be awake.

They sold him down the river. All of them.

Snakes. I knew Karen was—that wasn't no surprise. She knew I knew and Blaze knew I knew and I reckon Blaze knew it himself even when they was all loved up. She got cold blood in them veins and that was the first thing came out of her mouth straightaway—*It wasn't me, it was all him, I ain't done nothing*—even though she was the one from the start pushing him on—wanting more—wanting blood—shouting *get him* 'cause she wanted the guy stabbed. I heard it and I ain't forgot—but she just blabs to the feds straight off—just total lies, unbelievable. And that's her man she's chatting about, so imagine what she says about me.

So the mayor lied to Blaze—what d'you expect? All them people's liars, there's no point wanting anything different. But when you got a crew and they're your people you got to stand together—'cause if you're not for each other, who else is? Nobody else never stood up for us—not parents, not teachers, not social workers, not nobody—so all we got is each other and if that don't count for nothing, then we're just alone and we're fucked.

This is how it always ends for people like us anyway. They get us eventually—it's just a question of how and when. Pointless trying to make things end different, 'cause they won't. If you got your eyes open you see what's around you—you know where you're headed, so why fight it? From day one the people that run shit just want you to disappear—and they got a place to make you disappear into as well. So when they get you, you got to stand together.

At least that's what I thought until I'm in the back of the van with Lee and Femi, and before we're even at the station they're both kicking off same as Karen outside the warehouse—blaming it all on Blaze—acting like they was pushed into it, like they was almost hostages, too.

I don't say nothing. I'm sitting there listening to them two chatting their poison and I'm thinking Blaze knew it—he knew we'd all be arrested—he didn't expect nothing from the mayor, but he was talking to us. He was telling us what to say and that's what Femi and Lee's doing—just doing what Blaze said—but I ain't that—I ain't no snake even if it's what Blaze wants. So I say nothing. I know my rights.

I say nothing, not in the van, not at the station, not in the cell, not to the batty lawyer they give me, not a word, not nothing. 'Cause I ain't a snake. Once you start talking to people like that, they can twist you up, make you say anything they want. Only thing is to keep it zipped.

And when the judge sends me down I won't say nothing neither, 'cause none of this is a surprise—the question wasn't never where I'd end up, it was always just when. And better for this than for stealing or some small shit. At least this was something real—at least me and Blaze stood together till the end—at least I made a mark—didn't just sink away and disappear like I never existed like what was expected of me.

Me and Blaze can be proud 'cause they didn't break us. We did our thing and after that we didn't even bend for them or nothing. And that's pure, man, that's real.

I seen the History Channel, there's always been people like us—people who have to live off whatever scraps is left after everyone else has helped themselves—but I done something about it. I stood up—went against the flow—made my mark. Ain't a lot of people can say that, but Blaze can and I can—so I'm proud of what I done and who I am.

You look around—you sit on the bus and look around at all the people—how many you going to see that can actually say they done something? Something real and loud and true that got noticed.

Everyone watching on TV—seeing me get cuffed and dragged off—they probably think I was shitting myself. Wasn't, though. I know what's next, but I always known that. I was born into a life where nothing I did made no difference—this is always where I was going to end up.

When I'm sent down I know the place will be full of psychos that'll stab you with a sharpened toothbrush if you look at them wrong, but I can handle myself. I handled myself all my life without no help from no one. And if they think it's a punishment that all the days is the same—Monday, Tuesday, Wednesday, on and on, no difference—that don't sound so bad to me. Breakfast, lunch, dinner all there for you every time. I ain't never had that—so how bad can it be? They got gyms in there and everything. I seen it before—people go in skinny, come out buff. I can do that.

I ain't an idiot. I know it's going to be a hard and a cold place and there's bad people in there that'll try to mess me up—but when I think about all them weeks in a row—every one the same—it don't scare me, not even a bit. I never known what's next—never from the day I was born—always been running, hiding, scrapping to keep myself safe. So it ain't no holiday, but it's a pause, ain't it—maybe a reset. I ain't afraid. And I don't regret nothing, neither.

Zombies, man—the world's full of zombies that take what's given to them even if it ain't worth having and never even complain. That ain't Blaze and it ain't me. We stood up. Might seem like it didn't get us nowhere, but at least we did it.

I been news. I been famous. Whatever happens to me now—whatever dump they send me to—I always got that. I had my moment.

Acknowledgments

I would like to thank the consultant child and adolescent psychiatrist Dr. Iain McClure, for alerting me to the subject of ADHD, guiding my reading on the topic, and giving me unstinting advice throughout the writing process. Any errors are entirely my own.

For allowing me to quote from their books, which were invaluable in researching this novel, I would like to thank Matthew Smith (*Hyperactive: The Controversial History of ADHD*), Sami Timimi (*Naughty Boys: Anti-Social Behaviour, ADHD and the Role of Culture*), Steven Rose (*The 21st Century Brain: Explaining, Mending and Manipulating the Mind*), and Harriet Sergeant (*Among the Hoods: My Years with a Teenage Gang*). *Reading the Riots: Investigating England's Summer of Disorder*, edited by Dan Roberts, was also an important source.

I would like to thank the former staff of the now defunct Camden Mentoring Plus, and also Darren, who taught me far more than I taught him. Thank you also to First Story, for my placement in a south London school.

I owe particular thanks and gratitude to Rebecca McNally at Bloomsbury, and also to Emma Bradshaw, Laura Brooke, and Emily Sweet.

Thanks also to Richard Sved and John and Susan Sutcliffe, and to my goddaughter, Esther McRae, for providing a twenty-four-hour dialogue consultancy by text message service.

Above all, for more than I could ever explain, thank you, Maggie O'Farrell.

PERMISSIONS

Extract on page 179 from Elist, Jasmine, *Bronwen Hruska talks parenting pressure, ADD and 'Accelerated'*, 2012, *LA Times*. Reproduced with kind permission Jasmine Elist.

Extract on page 211 from 'Side-effects for Ritalin listed as 'common' or 'very common', electronic Medicines Compendium (eMC), 2015

Extract on page 218 from 'Share of the Week', Barclays Stockbrokers, March 3, 2014, www.barclaysstockbrokers. co.uk/Market-Insight/Analysis/Pages/share-of-the-week. aspx (content no longer accessible at this site)

Lichtenstein, P., Halldner, L., Zetterqvist, J., Sjölander, A., Serlachius, E., Fazel, S., . . . Larsson, H. (2012). Medication for attention deficit–hyperactivity disorder and criminality. *N Engl J Med*, *367*(21), 2006–2014. doi:10.1056/NEJMoa1203241

Extract on page 238 from Davies, James, *Cracked: Why Psychiatry Is Doing More Harm Than Good*, 2013, reproduced with kind permission of Icon Books Ltd

The author and publisher gratefully acknowledge the permissions granted to reproduce the third party copyright materials contained in this book. Every effort has been made to trace copyright holders and to obtain their written permission for the use of copyright material. The author and publisher apologize for any errors or omissions in the copyright acknowledgments contained in this book, and would be grateful if notified of any corrections that should be incorporated in future reprints or editions of this book.

All tweets in the novel are fictional.